哈福

哈福

30秒破解英語會話！

Speaking Naturally

30秒用英語和老外聊不停，超簡單！

施孝昌
Scott Williams 合著

英語會話速成58公式
30秒用英語聊不停

附贈光碟
MP3

3大保證

1 讓您學英語，和學中文一樣簡單
2 讓你能在短短30秒，學會講道地英語
3 讓你30秒征服，英語會話必備1000句

只要您具有中學3年的英語程度，
你一定辦得到！

學英語，和學中文一樣簡單

　　學英語，只要用對方法，其實和學中文一樣簡單。學英語和學走路一樣，必須按部就班地來。單字當然要記，文法規則當然要學，但是國中、高中所記的單字和文法規則，已經足夠，為什麼說起英語，還是不流利、不自然呢？

　　語言的學習是自然的，英語該怎麼說、我們就跟著怎麼說、而不是一字一套單字和文法，硬把中文翻成英文，要如何才能自然、流利的說英語呢？那就是本書要教您的秘訣了。學會講純正的英語！

　　Q：30秒可以學會講英語，真的嗎？

　　A：假如你具有中學三年英語的程度，你大可不必懷疑，你絕對可以在30秒內開口說英語。

　　「如果30秒可以學會講英語，為什麼我學了這麼多年英語，還是不會講？」你也許會這麼問。

　　在回答這個問題之前，我們先來看幾個例子，然後你再決定，有了一本好的教材，你是不是可以在30秒學會講英語。

　　首先，你看下列這些英文單字，有沒有難字，你是不是都很熟悉？

am	are	is		
not				
I	me	you	it	this
does	will			
with				
cut	take			

　　接著，我們來看一下在這個世界裡，實際生活中，如何講英語：

　　（一）與朋友聊天時、上課中、聽簡報等，有人在解釋一個問題給你聽，你聽不明白，你要跟對方說：「對不起，我聽糊塗了，

不明白你在説什麼。」怎麼説？

（二）你逛街、到百貨公司、地攤等去購物，店員給你看了好幾樣東西，你選定了式樣、價格、顏色都很合你意的一項，你要説：「我決定要買這個。」怎麼説？

（三）你是公司的主管，你要部屬擬一份公文、企劃、報告等文件，他交上來了，你一看，唉呀，寫的什麼東西啊？整份文件漏洞百出，你把他召來，他説：「什麼事？」你拿起文件，要跟他説：「你這份東西不完整，研究不深入！」怎麼説？

這三句話用英語該怎麼説？你會不會説？你需要想多久才能勉強「囁嚅」出口，還生怕對方聽不懂？

不用怕，你如果認識上面所列的單字，你可以在30秒學會全部這三句話！Yes, 只要30秒！

（一）我聽糊塗了，不明白你在説什麼。

　　　I am not with you.

（二）我決定買這個。

　　　I'll take it.

（三）這份東西不完整，研究不深入。

　　　This does not cut it.

你看，是不是很簡單？

上面這三句話，分別在本書的Unit 9，Unit 17，Unit 41。

再來，假如你知道I am not with you.是「我不明白你在説什麼？」那當你有機會解釋一件事情給別人聽，或做簡報時，你能不能用標準英語很漂亮地問聽眾，「你們聽懂嗎？」Are you ＿＿＿＿＿＿?對了，就是Are you with me?

不論你自認是英語的初學者，或是中、高級的學習者，本書要教你的英語，就是這樣標準，這樣簡單，這樣容易學習！

本書特色與使用方法

　　本書是美國AA Bridgers.公司所製作的英語教材，其基本特色是純正美語，沒有台客英語，用字很簡單，能讓你用早已學會的英文基本單字，在最短時間內，開口表達你的意思。

　　另外，本書歸納了實際生活的各種場合，最常用的1000句以上的英語，將每一句的使用時機，使用方法，注意要點，以最精緻、最容易學習的方式表現出來，讓你的每個30秒都能真正學到有用的英語，並且能夠舉一反三，自己隨心所欲地造句。

　　「實用例句」則依照每種場合所可能用到的句子全部列出來，讓你在每一種場合，都能用最有深度、最富變化的英語來表達活生生的你，而不是平板的，僵硬的，背誦式的英文。

　　英語的學習，非常注重發音和語調，不正確的發音，讓人不知所云。本書將重要的單字，依照美國人一般講話時的發音和重音，以標準KK音標注音，就是要讓你講出來的語音，跟美國人一樣順。

　　你最好的學習法是跟著MP3老師的示範學習，因為說話是有語調的。語調是一種喜怒哀樂的情緒綜合表現，說話時語調不協調，會造成你要表達的情緒不明，嚴重減低你的溝通效果，所以，跟著專業老師錄製的音調學習，效果最好。

　　其實，一個人如果花了很多時間，還是不能講英語，絕對是跟錯老師，用錯教材。而用了本書和AA Bridgers. 的英語教材後，很快的，你的聽力就會進步神速，你的朋友，特別是外國朋友，會很訝異你的英語為什麼說得這麼「美國」，這麼「溜」！你就再「溜」一口純正的英語給他們聽吧！

Chapter 6　社交英語

Chapter 7　徵詢英語

Chapter 8　需要協助時

Chapter 9　英語會話詢問篇

Chapter

1

打招呼

朋友間見面如何打招呼

Dialogue 1

A Hey John, how are you?
嘿，約翰，你好嗎？

B Not so good.
不怎麼好。

A Why's that?
怎麼了？

B Well, my mom is sick.
唉，我媽病了。

I don't have enough money to buy her any medicine.
我不夠錢給她買藥。

A I could let you borrow some money if you'd like.
如果你要的話，我可以讓你借點錢。

B That would be great.　Thanks a lot.
那太好了。很謝謝你。

Chapter 1

會話 2 **Dialogue 2**

Ⓐ Hi Mary, what's going on?
嗨，瑪莉，妳都在做些什麼事啊？

Ⓑ Not a lot.
沒什麼重要的事啦。

What are you up to?
你呢？你怎樣？

Ⓐ I'm about to go to the bank.
我正要去銀行。

Ⓑ Would it be all right if I went with you?
我跟你去可以嗎？

I need to make a deposit.
我得去存款。

Ⓐ Sure, that would be fine.
當然可以，那沒問題的。

Ⓑ OK, let me get my wallet and we'll take off.
好，讓我拿一下我的錢包，我們就走。

30秒破解英語會話

　　我們在學習英語的時候，關於見面問好說法，最常學到的是How are you?（你好嗎？），但你要注意，How are you?不是英美人士見面時最常用的說法。

　　在美國，熟人見面最常說的是How are you doing?或

What's up?

　　How are you?是兩個萍水相逢的人彼此表示善意，互相問好的話。在熟人之間，則只有在一段時間沒有見面的情況之下，再度見面才會這麼說的。但若是兩個熟人已經有很長一段時間沒有見面，則也不會說How are you?，而會說How have you been?（你這一向可好？）。

　　Unit 7的「30秒破解英語會話」裡，對於What's up?的用法和應答，有詳細的解說。

　　在英、美等真正每天使用英語的國家，彼此很熟的朋友，尤其是年輕人、上班族見面時打招呼，常說的是What's going on?、What's up?或What are you up to?等比較輕鬆流行的招呼語。

舉一反三 **Useful Sentences**

⊃ 見面的招呼語

01 **Hey, how are you?**
嘿，你好嗎？

02 **How have you been?**
你這一向都好嗎？

03 **What's up?**
你好啊！

04 **What's new?**
有沒有什麼新聞啊？

05　I haven't seen you for ages.
我好久沒有見到你了。

06　It's been a long time.
咱們好久沒見了。

07　Long time no see.
好久沒見！

08　How are you doing?
你好嗎？

09　Hello.
你好！

10　Hi.
嗨，你好。

⊃ 說再見

01　Have a nice night.
祝你今晚愉快。

02　Have a nice weekend.
祝你週末快樂。

03　Talk to you later.
再說了，再見。

04　See you later.
待會見。

05　I'll be seeing you.
再見。

06	**See you around.** 回頭見。
07	**Bye. Catch you later.** 再見了，回頭再見。
08	**Take care.** 保重。
09	**See you soon.** 再會。
10	**Bye.** 再見。

重要英語單字　Vocabulary

ages [ˈedʒɪz] → （口語）很長的一段時間

medicine [ˈmɛdəsn̩] →藥

bank [bæŋk] →銀行

deposit [dɪˈpɑzɪt] →存款

wallet [ˈwɑlɪt] →皮包

如何跟新認識的朋友打招呼

會話 1 **Dialogue 1**

MP3 3

A Hello, my name is John.
哈囉，妳好。我的名字叫約翰。

B Hi, I'm Mary.
嗨，你好，我是瑪莉。

Are you new in town?
你是新來本地的嗎？

A Yah, I just moved here.
是啊，我剛搬到這裡。

B Where are you from?
你是從哪裡來的？

A I grew up in Taiwan, but I was in New York for a couple of years.
我在台灣長大，不過在紐約待了兩年。

B Well, it's good to meet you.
是嗎，很高興遇見你。

Welcome to Los Angels.
歡迎到洛杉磯來。

會話 2 Dialogue 2

Ⓐ Excuse me. Haven't we met before?
對不起，我們以前好像見過面吧？

Ⓑ I don't think so.
我想沒有吧。

Ⓐ You work for IBM, don't you?
你不是在IBM上班嗎？

Ⓑ Yes, that's right.
是啊，沒錯。

Ⓐ I think I met you at Mr. Lin's party last Christmas.
我想我去年耶誕節在林先生的宴會上見過你。

Ⓑ Oh, really?
喔，真的嗎？

Ⓐ Well, anyway, my name's John.
是啊，不談它了。我的名字叫約翰。

Ⓑ I'm Mary.
我叫瑪莉。

Nice to meet you.
很榮幸認識你。

30秒破解英語會話

　　不管是在公司，在一般的聚會、宴會或是在住家附近，總會遇到原本不認識的人彼此自我介紹以便互相認識，想認識新朋友作自我介紹，英語的説法就是My name is ～.或是I am～.例如：你的名字是約翰(John)，你自我介紹時可以説I am John.或My name is John.

　　有人過來跟你作自我介紹，你要跟對方説「很高興認識你」，並告訴對方你叫什麼名字。

　　跟對方説「很高興認識你」的英語有以下幾種説法：It's good to meet you.、Glad to meet you.、Nice to meet you.、Pleased to meet you.或是簡單的説Hi。如何做自我介紹我們已經説過了，就是説My name is～.或I'm～.

舉一反三　Useful Sentences

⊃ 有人跟你自我介紹，你怎麼回答

01	How do you do? I'm Robert. 久仰，久仰。敝人名叫羅伯。
02	Pleased to meet you. I'm Jane. 很高興認識你，我叫珍恩。
03	It's good to meet you. I'm Robert. 認識你真好，我是羅伯。
04	Glad to meet you. I'm Jane. 很高興與您會面，我是珍恩。

05	Nice to meet you. I'm Robert. 很榮幸與你會面，我是羅伯。
06	Hi, I'm Elizabeth, but everyone calls me Lisa. 嗨，你好，我的名字是伊麗沙白，不過大家都叫我麗沙。

重要英語單字 Vocabulary

moved [muvd] →搬家（move的過去式）

town [taʊn] →城市

grew up →長大（grow up的過去式）

每天開口說一句

如何與陌生人搭訕

會話
1

Dialogue 1

Ⓐ Pardon me, do you have the time?
對不起，你知道現在幾點嗎？

Ⓑ It's 8:05.
現在是八點五分。

Ⓐ Do you know when the bus for Dallas leaves?
你知道到達拉斯的巴士幾點開嗎？

Ⓑ It leaves at 8:20.
八點二十開。

I'm taking that bus also.
我也是要搭那班巴士的。

Ⓐ Good, I thought I was late.
太好了，我還以為我來遲了呢。

I'm meeting my wife at 9:00.
我約好九點跟我太太見面。

Ⓑ I think you'll be just fine.
我想你沒有問題的啦。

會話 2 Dialogue 2

（在體育館觀賞球賽……）

Ⓐ Excuse me, could you tell me where the popcorn stand is?
對不起，可以請你告訴我賣爆米花的攤子在哪嗎？

Ⓑ Yes, it's right around the corner by section 3.
可以，就在拐角第三座位區旁邊。

Ⓐ OK, do you know how much popcorn is?
好，你知道爆玉米花的價錢是多少嗎？

Ⓑ For a large or small?
大杯的還是小杯的？

Ⓐ Large.
大的。

Ⓑ Large popcorn is \$3.50.
大杯爆玉米花是三塊五美元。

30秒破解英語會話

　　Excuse me.這句話的中文翻譯是「對不起」，但是要注意，美國人說Excuse me.這句話時，並不是真的在向對方道歉，而是用在要跟對方說話之前，先說Excuse me.以引起對方的注意，叫他知道你要跟他說話。

　　Unit 43所列的英語，才是真正表示道歉應該說的話，請參照。

Useful Sentences

舉一反三

● 與陌生人搭訕

01 Nice weather we're having.
天氣真好啊。

02 It's a beautiful day outside!
外頭的天氣真好！

03 Can you believe this weather?
你能相信天氣竟然這樣好（這樣壞）？

04 Pardon me, do you have the time?
對不起，您知道現在的時間嗎？

05 Excuse me, could you tell me where the station is?
對不起，可以請你告訴我車站在哪裡嗎？

06 Excuse me, where is the coke machine?
對不起，飲料販賣機在哪裡？

重要英語單字 Vocabulary

popcorn [ˈpɑpˈkɔrn]
→爆米花

stand [stænd] →小攤子

corner [ˈkɔrnɚ] →角落

section [ˈsɛkʃən] →區域

weather [ˈwɛðɚ] →天氣

pardon [ˈpɑrdən] →原諒

excuse [ɪkˈskjus] →對不起

station [ˈsteʃən] →車站

machine [məˈʃin] →機器

coke machine →飲料自動販賣機

如何跟要遠離的親友道別

Dialogue 1

Ⓐ Well Tom, I hope you have a good time in America.

就這樣了，湯姆。我希望你在美國玩得很愉快。

I'll miss you.

我會想你的。

Ⓑ I'll miss you too.

我也會想你的。

You mean a lot to me.

你在我心中的地位是很重要的。

Ⓐ I'll write if you will.

我會給你寫信，你也要寫噢。

Ⓑ You bet!

當然！

Ⓐ Here's $2000 for the trip.

這裡是二千美元，給你當旅費。

Use some of it for stamps.

要把一些用來買郵票啊！

Ⓑ Thanks a lot.　Bye.

多謝，再見。

Chapter 1

會話 2 Dialogue 2

Ⓐ Mary , we're going to miss you.
　瑪莉啊，我們會很想你的。

Ⓑ I'll miss you too.
　我也會很想你們。

Ⓐ We can write letters. It's cheaper than calling.
　我們可以寫信就好，那比打電話便宜。

Ⓑ I will, but I'll probably call too.
　我會寫的，我或許也會打電話。

Ⓐ OK. Do you know when you'll come and visit?
　好吧。你知道幾時還會再來拜訪我們嗎？

Ⓑ Of course, I'll visit at least once a year, maybe more.
　當然，我最少每年會來拜訪一次，也許更多次。

30秒破解英語會話

有人要遠離，你一定得跟他説的話就是I'll miss you.
You bet.是一句口語，表示「當然，沒問題」的意思。

重要英語單字 Vocabulary

miss [mɪs] →想念
mean [min] →意義
stamp [stæmp] →郵票

probably [ˈprɑbəblɪ]
→可能的
at least →至少

Unit 5

在宴會上

（宴會上與主人道別……）

Ⓐ Thanks a lot for having us.
真感謝你邀請我們來。

We had a good time.
我們玩得很愉快。

Ⓑ I'm glad you came.
我很高興你們來。

You're welcome any time.
隨時都歡迎你們來。

Ⓐ Congratulations again on your promotion.
再度恭喜你高昇。

You deserve it.
你是得之無愧的。

Ⓑ Thanks. I'll see you Monday at the office.
謝謝。咱們星期一辦公室再見了。

Ⓐ OK. Bye the way, tell your wife she throws a great party.

好。還有，請告訴你夫人，她辦了一個很成功的宴會。

Ⓑ I will. **See you later.**

我會告訴她的。再見！

會話
2   **Dialogue 2**

（在宴會中……）

Ⓐ Hi, I'm Mary.

嗨，我叫瑪莉。

Ⓑ I'm John.

我是約翰。

Ⓐ **Would you like some cake?**

你要吃點蛋糕嗎？

I made it myself.

是我自己做的。

Ⓑ Absolutely. Mmmm, this is good.

肯定要嚐嚐！嗯…，真好吃。

Ⓐ Thanks, would you like to dance?

謝謝，你要跳支舞嗎？

Ⓑ OK, but you may have to lead, I'm not a great dancer.

好，不過可能要由妳來帶舞，因我跳得不好。

30秒破解英語會話

　　你去參加宴會，離開前要先謝謝主人邀請你來參加宴會，如:Thank you for inviting me.等等，如果你是與你的另一半一起去，要説：Thank you for having us.接下去再跟主人説「我們玩得很愉快(We had a good time.)」

舉一反三　**Useful Sentences**

⊃ 謝謝主人的邀請

01　Thank you for having us.
謝謝你邀請我們來。

02　Thanks a lot for having us.
很感謝您讓我們來參加。

03　Thank you for inviting me.
謝謝你邀我來參加。

04　Thank you for inviting us.
謝謝你邀我們來參加。

⊃ 宴會後的道別語

01　I had a good time.
我玩得很愉快。

02　I had a lovely time.
我度過了一段美好的時光。

03 I had a nice time.
我玩得很盡興。

04 Thank you for a lovely evening.
謝謝你給我一個美好的夜晚。

05 Thank you for a nice evening.
謝謝你，今晚真盡興。

重要英語單字 Vocabulary

congratulations →[kən͵grætʃəˈleʃənz] →恭喜

promotion [prəˈmoʃən] →升遷

deserve [dɪˈzɝv] →應得的；得之無愧的

throw [θro] →舉辦（宴會）

lead [lid] →主導

每天開口說一句

家人回家來，如何招呼他

會話 1 Dialogue 1

（放學回到家⋯⋯）

Ⓐ Hi, Mom.
嗨，媽。

Ⓑ Hi John. How was school?
嗨，約翰，今天上學還好嗎？

Ⓐ It was fun.
好玩！

Mrs. Lee showed us how to do science experiments.
李老師教我們怎麼做科學實驗。

Ⓑ Wow, what did you do?
喔，你們做什麼實驗？

Ⓐ We did an experiment with water.
我們用水做了一項實驗。

We boiled it and it evaporated.
我們把它煮滾，它就蒸發了。

It was neat.
太棒了。

B Well, that sounds like fun.

嗯，那聽起來很好玩的樣子。

I am glad you liked it.

我很高興你喜歡學校的實驗。

會話 2 Dialogue 2

A Hi honey, **I'm home.**

嗨，親愛的，我回來了。

B Hi sweetie. How was your day?

嗨，老公。你今天上班還好吧？

A Pretty normal.

普通啦。

Nothing exciting happened.

沒什麼特別緊張的事發生。

How are you?

那妳好嗎？

B Great! Mary just called and said she can baby-sit tonight.

很好。瑪莉剛打了電話來，說她今晚可以看小孩。

A All right!!!

好極了！

Let's go see a movie.

咱們看電影去。

B OK, this will be fun!

好啊，這滿好的。

We haven't been to a movie in a long time.

我們好久沒有去看電影了。

30秒破解英語會話

Let's go see a movie. 這是一句口語，在go和see這兩個動詞之間沒有看到文法上所說的「兩個動詞之間要有個to」，注意：這種用法是英語會話中常見的說法，例如：去拿個可樂(go get a coke)，去買些東西(go buy some stuffs)。

重要英語單字　Vocabulary

showed [ʃod] →展示

science [saɪns] →科學

experiment [ɪksˈpɛrəmənt] →實驗

boiled [ˈbɔɪld] →煮沸

evaporate [ɪˈvæpəˌret] →蒸發

sweetie →親愛的（夫婦相互間的暱稱）

normal [ˈnɔrml̩] →平凡

exciting [ikˈsaɪtɪŋ] →令人興奮的；叫人緊張的

baby-sit [ˈbebɪˌsɪt] →代看小孩

Unit 7

有客人來訪

（開門迎接客人……）

客：Hey Mary, what's up?
嘿，瑪莉，妳好啊？

主：Not much.
馬馬虎虎啦。

How was your trip?
你這一趟旅途還好吧？

客：Pretty good, but I got caught in a traffic jam in Atlanta.
很好，不過在亞特蘭大碰上了交通阻塞。

主：I'm really glad to see you.
我真高興看到你。

客：Yeah, it's been a long time.
是啊，好久沒見面了。

主：Too long.
太久了。

Have a seat and I'll get you a drink.
請坐，我來給你弄一杯飲料。

31

會話
2 **Dialogue 2**

（到岳父家接太太……）

Ⓐ Hi John.　How's our new son-in-law?
嗨，約翰。我們這個女婿還好吧？

Ⓑ I'm pretty good, but I left my bag at home by accident.
我很好，不過我不小心把我的行李遺忘在家裡了。

Ⓐ That's all right.
那沒關係。

We've got some clothes for you here.
我們這裡有些衣服可以給你穿。

Ⓑ OK.　Where's Jane?
那好。珍恩在哪裡？

Ⓐ She's at Mary's, but she's on her way home.
她去瑪莉家，不過已經在回家的路上了。

Ⓑ Good, I can't wait to see her!
好，我等不及要見她。

30秒破解英語會話

　　有人來訪，你可以用在第一單元裡學的招呼語跟對方問好。

　　注意：What's up?是標準英語最常用的問好的説法，也就是我們見面時常説的「你好啊！」的意思。但What's

up?字面上的原意是「近來有沒有什麼事啊？」，所以回答時不能直接說「我很好」、「不太好」，像I am fine.或Not too good.的說法，而要用Not much.來表示「沒什麼大事啦！」，也就是「馬馬虎虎」的意思。

　第一單元裡提到的招呼語很多，有些是一般的招呼語，有些是很熟的朋友間的招呼語，該怎麼用，第一單元裡已有詳述。

重要英語單字　Vocabulary

trip [trɪp] →旅遊

traffic [ˈtræfɪk] →交通

jam [dʒæm] →瓶頸

son-in-law →女婿

accident [ˈæksədənt] →意外

Chapter

2

基礎英語會話

會話 1 Dialogue 1

Ⓐ Mary, I'm Dr. Lin.
瑪莉，我是林博士。

I'm leading the class in English this semester.
這學期是我主授這門英文課。

Ⓑ Hello, sir. It's a pleasure to meet you.
先生，您好。很榮幸認識您。

Ⓐ I am originally from Taiwan, but I have traveled all over the world.
我原籍來自台灣，不過我已走遍全世界。

Ⓑ I haven't traveled much, so I know I have a lot to learn from you.
我不太出門旅遊，所以我知道我有很多可以從你那裡學習的。

Ⓐ I hope you enjoy the class.
我希望你喜歡這門課。

Ⓑ I think I will.
我想我會的。

I've already bought the textbook!
我連教科書都買了耶！

會話 2 Dialogue 2

Ⓐ John, I'd like you to meet my mother.
約翰，我要你見見我媽媽。

Ⓑ Hello, Mrs. Lee. Good to meet you.
妳好，李太太。與您會面真好。

Ⓐ It's good to meet you, John. You can call me Nancy.
約翰，與您見面真好。你可以叫我南西就行。

Ⓑ Are you sure?
妳真的覺得這樣可以嗎？

Ⓐ Of course I'm sure.
當然是真的。

Any friend of my son is a friend of mine.
我兒子的任何朋友也都是我的朋友。

And all of my friends call me Nancy.
而我所有的朋友都是叫我南西的。

Ⓑ OK, Mrs. Lee, I mean Nancy.
好吧，李太太……喔，我是說南西。

Chapter 2

30秒破解英語會話

　　要介紹兩個人彼此認識，英語會話中有幾種常見的說法。最直接的說法是「我要把妳介紹給某某人」I'd like to introduce you to某某人，較簡單的說法則是「我來介紹某某人」I'd like to introduce某某人。

　　假如你對被介紹的雙方都很熟，最客氣的說法則是對著一方說，I'd like you to meet某某人，這時你不用「介紹」introduce這樣正經八百的字眼，而用「見見」meet這樣親近的語言，表示「我要你見見某某人」。

舉一反三　**Useful Sentences**

● 自我介紹

01　Hi, I'm Dr. Lee.
　　嗨，我是李博士。

02　Hi, my name is David, and you are?
　　嗨，我的名字是大衛，你是……？

03　Hi, I'm John. What's your name?
　　嗨，我是約翰，你叫什麼名字？

● 介紹朋友彼此認識

01　I'd like to introduce you to John.
　　我想介紹你認識約翰。

02 John, this is Mary. Mary, this is John.
約翰，這位是瑪莉。瑪莉，這位是約翰。

03 Mr. Smith, I'd like to introduce a friend of mine.
史密斯先生，我想介紹我的一個朋友。

04 I'd like you to meet David.
我想要你見見大衛。

➲ **有人介紹另一個人跟你認識，你怎麼說**

01 How do you do?
久仰！

02 Glad to meet you.
很高興與您會面。

03 Nice to meet you.
真榮幸認識您。

04 Pleased to meet you.
很高興遇見您。

05 I've heard so much about you.
我聽過很多有關您的事。

06 Hi.
嗨，你好。

➲ 道別

01
Nice to meet you.
有幸認識您真好。

02
Good to meet you.
真榮幸認識您。

03
It was a pleasure meeting you.
與您會面，實屬榮幸。

04
I enjoyed meeting you.
能認識您我覺得很高興。

重要英語單字　Vocabulary

pleasure [ˈplɛʒɚ] →榮幸

semester [səˈmɛstɚ] →學期

originally [əˈrɪgɪnḷɪ] →原本

traveled [ˈtrævḷd] →旅遊（travel的過去分詞）

textbook [ˈtɛks͵bʊk] →教科書

introduce [͵ɪntrəˈdjus] →介紹

already [ɔlˈrɛdɪ] →已經

Unit 9
對方說的話你沒聽清楚，怎麼辦

會話 1 — Dialogue 1

MP3 10

Ⓐ Take a right at the stop light, then go left at B Street.

在紅綠燈的地方右轉，然後在B街左轉。

Oh, don't forget to get in the right lane so you can ...

噢，別忘記開在右車道上以便你能……

Ⓑ Hold on, I lost you.

停停，我讓你給弄糊塗了。

Please start over.

請再重新來過。

Ⓐ OK, right at the stop light and left at B Street......

好，在紅綠燈向右，B街向左……

Ⓑ Right at the stop light and left at B Street......

紅綠燈向右，B街向左……

Ⓐ Then get into the right lane and turn in right before the sign.

然後開在右車道上，就在號誌之前右轉進來。

B Good, I've got it.

好，我懂了。

Dialogue 2

會話
2

（學校檢討習題……）

A The answer for number 6 is C, 7 is B, 8 is A, 9 is D. . .

第六題答案是 C，第七是 B，八是 A，九是 D……

B Mrs. Lee, could you tell me what number 7 is again please?

李老師，妳能不能再告訴我第七題是什麼？

A Sure, 7 is B. Do you need any others?

當然可以，七是 B。你還需要其他的嗎？

B Yes, please, 8 and 9.

是的，請告訴我八和九。

A 8 is A, 9 is D.

八是 A，九是 D。

B Thank you.

謝謝你。

30秒破解英語會話

　　有時對方說的太快或是太小聲，以致於你沒聽清楚，要請對方重說一遍，大家可能都學過I beg your pardon?或Beg your pardon?這兩句話，那是很正式也很禮貌地，請對方把剛剛說的話重說一次。但是還有其他的說法，以下有詳列，當中的Run that by me again.是一句口語，學了之後，很自然地說出來，老美會覺得你的英語很棒。

舉一反三　**Useful Sentences**

➲ 告訴對方你沒聽清楚

01
I'm sorry, I'm not with you.
對不起，你的意思我聽不明白。

02
I didn't get that.
我不懂。

03
I didn't catch that.
我不太明白你說什麼。

04
I lost you.
我讓你給搞糊塗了。

05
Pardon me, I don't understand.
對不起，我不明白。

06
Hold on, I missed that.
停停，我沒聽見剛剛說什麼。

➲ 請對方重說一遍

01 I beg your pardon?
請你再說一遍。

02 Beg your pardon?
請你再說一遍。

03 Would you mind repeating what you just said?
請你把你剛說的再說一次，可以嗎？

04 Could you repeat what you just said?
妳能再複述妳剛說的話嗎？

05 Excuse me, could you repeat that?
對不起，妳能再重複一遍嗎？

06 Could you say that again?
你可以再說一次嗎？

07 Please start over.
請重新再來過一次？

08 Please say that again.
請再說一次。

09 Say that again.
再說一次。

10 How's that again?
再說一次，那是怎樣？

11 Run that by me again.
再把那回事跟我說一遍。

12 What did you say?
你剛說什麼？

| 13 | What?
什麼？ |

⊃ 請對方說慢一點

| 01 | I'm sorry, could you slow down please?
對不起，能請你慢一點嗎？ |
| 02 | Would you say that again more slowly, please?
請你再說一遍，慢一點。 |

⊃ 有人聽不清楚你說的話時

01	Sure, I'll repeat that. 當然，我再重複一次。
02	Oh, I'm sorry, let me say it again. 噢，對不起，讓我再說一遍。
03	OK, I'll start over. 好，我重新來過。
04	I'm sorry. Am I going too fast? 對不起，我說太快了嗎？

重要英語單字 Vocabulary

stop light（交通）紅綠燈

forget [fɚˈgɛt] →忘記

lane [len] →行車道

sign [saɪn] →號誌

answer [ˈænsɚ] →答案

 Dialogue 1

A Hi, David, this is Mary.

嗨，大衛，我是瑪莉。

B Hello.

喂。

A John and I would like you to come over this Saturday for a party.

約翰和我想請你本週六來我們家參加宴會。

B OK, I'd love to come.

好，我很樂意來參加。

A Great! It's this Saturday at 8.

好極了，宴會在本週六八點。

See you there.

咱們宴會上見。

B Sounds good.

很好。

I'll be there at 8.

我八點會到。

會話 2 Dialogue 2

A Mary, this is John.
瑪莉，我是約翰。

B Hi, John.
嗨，約翰。

A Are you doing anything Friday?
妳星期五有沒有什麼事？

B No.
沒有。

A Would you like to go see a movie with me?
妳要不要跟我去看場電影？

B Yes, I'd love to.
好啊，我很樂意去。

30秒破解英語會話

　　你要邀請朋友來你家作客，除非你正好遇上對方，否則就得打電話去邀請。電話中要告訴對方你的名字，一定要說This is + 你的名字，盡量不要說I am某某人，這是電話英語的規矩。

舉一反三 Useful Sentences

⊃ **提出邀請**

01 Would you like to come over?
妳要不要來我家？

02 Do you want to do something tonight?
妳今晚要不要做什麼事？

03 Are you busy today?
你今天忙不忙？

04 What are you doing tomorrow?
妳明天有什麼事要做？

05 Can you come to a party tonight?
你今晚能不能來參加宴會？

➲ 接受邀請

01 Sure, I'd love to.
當然，我很樂意。

02 OK, that will be fun.
好，那會很好玩。

03 You bet. What time?
當然要了。幾點？

04 Sure, what do you want to do?
好啊，你要做什麼？

05 Sounds good.
好啊。

➲ 問需要帶什麼東西

01 I wonder if I might be able to bring something?
我在想有什麼東西是我可以帶來的？

02 Is there anything I could bring?
有沒有什麼東西是我可以帶來的？

03 **What shall I bring?**
要我帶什麼東西來？

04 **Can I bring Cokes?**
我帶可樂來，可以嗎？

05 **What should I bring?**
要我帶什麼呢？

⊃ **對方要帶東西來，你怎麼回答**

01 **It's enough just to have you come.**
你人來就夠了。

02 **Oh, you don't need to.**
噢，你不用帶來。

03 **Just bring yourself.**
你人來就好了。

04 **Well, thanks, if you'd like to.**
是麼，謝了，如果你要帶，就帶吧。

05 **Well, Mary's bringing drinks, so why don't you bring salad?**
是麼，瑪莉要帶飲料，那你何不帶沙拉來？

重要英語單字 Vocabulary

yourself [jʊrˋsɛlf]
→你自己

bring yourself
→自己來參加

enough [ɪˋnʌf] →足夠的

drink [drɪŋk] →飲料

salad [ˋsæləd] →沙拉

Unit 11
如何拒絕對方的邀約

 Dialogue 1

ⓐ Mary, would you like to come over tomorrow?
瑪莉，妳明天要不要到我家來？

ⓑ Huh, tomorrow?
嗄，明天？

I have a doctor's appointment in the afternoon.
我明天下午跟醫生約好了。

ⓐ When is that?
那是幾點？

ⓑ At 3, but I have to leave by 2:30 to get there on time.
三點，不過我兩點半必須離開，才能準時到那裡。

I guess I'll have to pass.
我想我得錯過這回了。

ⓐ Well, maybe you could come next week some time.
是麼，也許妳可以下個星期的某個時候來。

ⓑ Sure, **give me a call and we'll get together.**
當然，給我打電話，我們聚聚。

會話 2 Dialogue 2

Ⓐ Hey Mary, are you doing anything tomorrow?
嘿，瑪莉，明天有沒有什麼事做？

Ⓑ At what time?
幾點？

Ⓐ About 6, I'm grilling burgers.
六點。我要炭烤漢堡。
I thought you and John might like to come over.
我想妳和約翰或許會願意過來。

Ⓑ I'd love to, but I have to study for a test tomorrow night.
我是想過來，不過我明晚有個考試，得讀書。
Thanks for asking.
謝謝你的邀請。

Ⓐ Maybe you could come over next time.
那也許下回你們可以來。
Good luck on your test.
祝你考試順利。

Ⓑ Thanks.
謝謝。

30秒破解英語會話

　　說到一件你已經決定好要做的事，它的句型是「I am + 現在分詞」，例如：在對話二，B已經決定隔天要烤漢堡 (grill burgers)，他打電話邀請瑪莉和約翰過來，在電話中他告訴瑪莉「我將要烤漢堡」，把grill改成現在分詞，說法就是I am grilling burgers。

Chapter 2

舉一反三 Useful Sentences

➲ 不能赴宴

01	I'm sorry, I can't. 對不起，我不行。
02	No, not tonight. 不，今晚不行。
03	I'd love to, but I have to work. 我很想去，但我得上班。
04	Thanks for the invitation, but I have other plans. 謝謝你的邀請，但我另外有約。
05	I'll have to pass. 這回我得錯過了。

重要英語單字 Vocabulary

appointment [əˈpɔɪntmənt] →約會
pass [pæs] →不參加
grill [grɪl] →（在烤架上）炭烤
burger [ˈbɝgɚ] →漢堡
invitation [ˌɪnvəˈteʃən] →邀請
plan [plæn] →計畫

Unit 12
如何用英語表達謝意

（借照相機……）

Ⓐ John, thanks a lot for the camera.
約翰，很感謝你的照相機。

It will definitely come in handy.
有了它，一定派得上用處，很方便。

Ⓑ Sure thing.
不用掛齒。

You really need a camera when you're on vacation.
人在度假的時候，總需要一個照相機的。

Ⓐ I wonder what type of film will be the best.
我在想，哪一型的底片最好？

Ⓑ I would get Kodak Gold 100 film since you're going to Hawaii.
既然妳是要到夏威夷，我會買柯達Gold 100的底片。

Ⓐ Wow, you're a lot of help.
唉呀，你真是幫了個大忙。

Thanks so much.
非常非常感謝。

B Any time.

不用客氣。

Have fun on your trip!

祝你旅途其樂無窮！

（宴會結束，主人付錢給表演的人……）

主：Thank you so much for coming tonight.

非常謝謝你今晚來表演。

Everyone really enjoyed your card tricks.

每個人都很喜歡你的紙牌魔術。

演：Thanks for having me.

謝謝你邀我來。

I'm glad I could help.

我很高興我能略盡薄能。

主：You definitely were a great help.

你的協助確實很大。

Here's the check.

這是支票。

I included a little extra for you.

我額外加了一點給你。

演：**You didn't have to do that!**
你不用這麼做的！

主：I know, but you were really great.
我知道，但你實在表演真好。

You deserve it.
你得之無愧。

演：Thanks a lot.　You're very kind.
謝謝你，你做人真好。

<figure>舉一反三</figure> **Useful Sentences**

➔ **如何用英語表達謝意**

01
Thanks a lot.
很感謝。

02
I appreciate the gift.
我很感謝你的禮物。

03
Thanks for helping.
謝謝你幫忙。

04
I'm really glad you helped us.
承蒙協助，實在很感激。

05
You were such a help.
你的協助實在太大了。

06 Thank you so much.
非常非常謝謝。

07 Thanks.
謝了。

➲ **有人跟你致謝時**

01 You bet.
沒問題。

02 Any time.
別客氣。

03 Sure, I'm glad to help.
當然，我樂意幫忙的。

04 You're welcome.
不客氣。

重要英語單字 Vocabulary

come in handy →派得上用處

definitely ['dɛfənətlɪ] →一定地；肯定地

camera ['kæmərə] →相機

film [fɪlm] →底片

trick [trɪk] →把戲

check →支票

include [ɪn'klud] →包括

extra ['ɛkstrə] →額外的

deserve [dɪ'zɝv] →應得的

Unit 13
如何用英語誇獎別人

會話 **1** Dialogue 1

MP3 14

Ⓐ Mary, **your hair looks great!**
瑪莉，妳的頭髮看起來好棒！

Did you go to a salon?
妳上髮廊了？

Ⓑ No, I fixed it myself.
沒有，我自個兒打理的。

Ⓐ You did? **That looks incredible!**
妳打理的？那看起來簡直是難以相信的好。

Ⓑ Thanks. I wanted to look good for my brother's wedding.
謝了。我哥哥的婚禮，我要弄得好看才好。

Ⓐ **Well, it worked.**
是麼，那很成功噢。

You look really good.
妳看起來真好看。

Ⓑ Thanks a lot.
很謝謝你。

會話 2 **Dialogue 2**

Ⓐ This cake is great!
這個蛋糕真好。

Ⓑ Thanks. I made it for you.
謝謝,我是為你作的。

Ⓐ Will you make it again some time?
妳幾時能不能再作?

Ⓑ Sure. Whenever you want.
當然。你幾時想吃都可以。

Ⓐ Really? **You're awesome.**
真的?妳太棒了。

How about tomorrow?
明天就作,怎麼樣?

Ⓑ Tomorrow? **Tomorrow it is!**
明天?明天就明天!

Anything for you.
為了你做什麼都可以!

30秒破解英語會話

　　逢人說幾句讚美的話,對方一定覺得很受用,英語會話中讚美的話不外乎,「你的某件東西好美、好棒」,或「我好喜歡你的某某東西」,例如:You hair looks great. 或I just love your hair.,以下有詳列更多,你可以選你認為較順口的記住一兩句就行。

舉一
反三 **Useful Sentences**

➲ 讚美對方

01 **Your hair looks great.**
妳的頭髮看起來真好。

02 **I just love your dress.**
我好喜歡妳這件套裝。

03 **The chicken is delicious.**
這個雞作得太好吃了。

04 **I really like your earrings.**
我真喜歡妳的耳環。

05 **This cake is super.**
這個蛋糕太棒太棒了！

06 **You look great!**
妳看起來真好看。

07 **You did a wonderful job.**
你表現得真好。

08 **I like the book.**
我喜歡這本書。

09 **I enjoyed your performance.**
我喜歡你的表演。

10 **That's very nice.**
那真好！

| 11 | That's nice.
那很好。 |

⊃ 有人讚美你時

01	Thank you. It's nice of you to say so. 謝謝，你這樣説真客氣。
02	Thank you, but it really isn't anything special. 謝謝你，不過那實在也沒什麼特殊的。
03	Thank you. Yours is even nicer. 謝謝你。妳自己的更好呢！
04	I'm glad you liked it. 我很高興你喜歡它。
05	Thank you. 謝謝你。
06	Thanks. 謝了。

重要英語單字 Vocabulary

salon [sə'lon] →髮廊

fixed [fɪkst] →（fix的過去式）打理

incredible [ɪn'krɛdəbl̩] →（口語）很棒的

wedding ['wɛdɪŋ] →婚禮

Unit 14
如何讓對方知道你想跟他說話

 Dialogue 1

A Excuse me, Mr. Lin.
對不起，林先生。

B Yes? What can I do for you?
什麼事？有事可為妳服務嗎？

A I need some batteries for my clock.
我的鐘需要電池。

B Are they out of power?
你的電池沒電了嗎？

A No, the batteries are missing.
不，電池不見了。

Maybe they got lost while we were moving our supplies.
也許我們在搬用品的時候，電池弄丟了。

B OK, check with Tom.
好吧，跟湯姆問一下。

He has the batteries.
他有電池。

A Thanks a lot.
很謝謝你。

會話 2 **Dialogue 2**

Ⓐ Excuse me, Mary, I'm sorry to interrupt you, but I need to ask you a question.

對不起，瑪莉。很抱歉打斷妳，不過我得問妳一個問題。

Ⓑ Sure, what is it?

當然，什麼問題？

Ⓐ Jane just called and said she has a flat tire.

珍恩剛打電話，說她車胎破了。

Could I borrow your car to go change her tire?

我可以借妳的車去幫她換車胎嗎？

Ⓑ Of course. The keys are on the table.

當然。鑰匙在桌上。

Ⓐ OK, thanks. Sorry to interrupt.

好，謝了。抱歉打斷妳了。

Ⓑ Don't worry about it.

別掛意。

Just go fix that tire.

去換車胎吧。

30秒破解英語會話

　　當你想要跟某人說話，想先叫他一聲，英語較正式的說法是Pardon me.或Excuse me.這兩句話只是用來引起對方的注意，並沒有「對不起」的意思。

Chapter 2

注意，英語在呼喚對方的注意之後，通常會接but這個字，你在説英語的時候，少了這個but的字，聽起來就不像是標準英語。

當有人叫你，表示有話想跟你説時，你的回答最正式的説法是Yes, What can I do for you?或是Yes? Can I help you?較簡單的回答是Yes?或Yeah?

有人打斷你跟別人的談話，他大半會先跟你説聲「對不起」，你的回答是It's all right.或是It's OK.

舉一
反三　**Useful Sentences**

◯ 你想跟某人說話時

01　Pardon me, Mr. Kim.
對不起，金先生。

02　Excuse me, Mary.
對不起，瑪莉。

03　Ma'am?
小姐！

04　Sir?
先生！

05　Waiter?
招待！

06　Hey, Mary.
喂，瑪莉。

⊃ 打岔

01 Pardon me, but...
抱歉，我……

02 I'm sorry to interrupt you, but . . .
我很抱歉打斷你，不過……

03 I hate to interrupt, but...
我實在不願打岔，但……

04 I'm sorry, but...
抱歉，我……

05 Excuse me, but...
對不起啊，我……

06 Oh, were you in the middle of something?
啊，你是不是正好有事做到一半？

07 Am I interrupting?
我打斷你了嗎？

重要英語單字　Vocabulary

batteries [ˈbætərɪz] →電池（battery的複數）
clock [klɑk] →時鐘
power [ˈpauɚ] →電力
missing [ˈmɪsɪŋ] →不見了
supplies [səˈplaɪz] →用品
flat tire →輪胎破了
tire [taɪr] →輪胎
interrupt [ˌɪntəˈrʌpt] →打斷：打岔
middle [ˈmɪdl̩] →中間

Chapter

3

英語會話更進一步

詢問電影或表演的時間

Dialogue 1

A Thank you for calling Movies 6.
謝謝你打電話來『Movie 6』電影院。

Can I help you?
能為你服務嗎？

B What time does Star Trek start?
『星艦迷航記』幾點開演？

A 6:00 and 7:40.
六點和七點四十。

B How much are tickets?
票價多少？

A For the early show they are $2.50.
早場是二塊五美元。

And for the late show they are $3.25.
晚場是三塊二毛五美元。

B OK, thank you very much.
好，非常謝謝你。

會話 2 **Dialogue 2**

Ⓐ John, this is Mary.
約翰，我是瑪莉。

Do you know when the football game starts?
你知道美式足球賽幾點開打嗎？

Ⓑ It starts at 3:00.
三點開打。

Do you want to go?
妳要去嗎？

Ⓐ Yes. Are we all riding together?
要。我們全部人都坐一部車去嗎？

Ⓑ No, we're going in our own cars.
不，我們要開我們自己的車去。

Ⓐ Well, could I ride with you?
那，我能不能坐你的車去？

I'll pay for parking.
我來付停車費。

Ⓑ Sure. Meet me here at 1:30.
好。一點半在這裡跟我碰面。

30秒破解英語會話

show當動詞可以做「放映、上演」的意思，例如：The local theater is showing Tom Cruise's latest picture.（本地的戲院正在放映湯姆克魯斯最近的電影。），或者你打電話到戲院問：「你們這個星期演哪一部電影？」，英語就是What are you showing this week?

show當名詞可以做「一場電影」的意思，所以說「早場的電影票價是250元」，這句話中的早場電影，英語就是the early show.

舉一反三　Useful Sentences

➲ 詢問資訊

01
What are you showing this week?
你們這星期演什麼？

02
What time does Star Wars start?
『星際大戰』幾點開演？

03
How much is a ticket?
一張票多少錢？

04
When does the program start?
這個節目什麼時候開始？

05
When does the football game start?
這場美式足球賽什麼時候開打？

06 Where is the rest room?
洗手間在哪裡？

➲ 問現在幾點

01 Do you have the time?
妳知道現在幾點嗎？

02 What time is it?
現在幾點？

➲ 問店裡營業的時間

01 What are your hours?
你們營業時間從幾點到幾點？

02 Could you tell me your hours?
可以告訴我你們的營業時間嗎？

03 Can you please tell me when you close?
請你告訴我你們幾點打烊？

重要英語單字 Vocabulary

program [ˈprogræm] →節目
game [gem] →（球類）比賽
parking [ˈparkɪŋ] →停車；泊車
hours [aʊrz] →（商店）營業時間
close [kloz] →（商店）打烊

Unit 16
· · · · · · · · · ·
詢問產品

Dialogue 1

Ⓐ What equipment does this car have?
這部車有什麼配備？

Ⓑ This car has the Power Package.
這部車有『自動動力套件』。

Are you familiar with that package?
你對這個套件熟嗎？

Ⓐ **Not really.**
不熟。

Ⓑ OK, the Power Package includes power windows and locks, power mirrors, and a power antenna.
好，這個套件包含自動窗、自動鎖、自動鏡和自動天線。

This particular car also has air conditioning and a CD player.
我們談的這部車還有冷氣和一個CD播放機。

會話 2 Dialogue 2

Ⓐ Do you have any toasters on sale?
你們的烤麵包機有在打折嗎？

Ⓑ Yes, we have three on sale.
有，我們有三型正在打折。

They are right over here.
它們都在這裡。

Ⓐ I want one that holds 4 pieces of bread.
我要一種可以裝四片麵包的。

Ⓑ Hmm, all of our sale toasters hold 2 pieces.
嗯，所有我們正在打折的烤麵包機都只能裝兩片。

But, we have a toaster that holds 4 pieces of bread that is actually less expensive than all three of these.
不過，我們有一型烤麵包機可以裝四片，而價格實際上要比全部這三型都便宜。

Ⓐ Can I see it?
可以讓我看看嗎？

Ⓑ Sure, I'd be happy to show it to you.
當然了，我很樂意把它展示給你看。

舉一
反三　**Useful Sentences**

● 詢問產品性能的問法

01
Tell me about this car.
告訴我有關這部車的性能。

02
What about this feature?
這個性能特點是什麼？

03
Could you explain that to me, please?
能否請你將那個解釋給我聽？

04
How do you fix this tire?
這種車胎要怎麼修？

05
Do you have any cars available?
你們有車賣嗎？

06
Could you tell me about your car?
可以講講你們的車給我聽嗎？

重要英語單字　**Vocabulary**

equipment [ɪˈkwɪpmənt] →配備

familiar [fəˈmɪljɚ] →熟悉

package [ˈpækɪdʒ] →套件；成套設備

power [ˈpauɚ] →動力

toaster [ˈtostɚ] →烤麵包機

particular [pɚˈtɪkjələ] →特定的；指定的

air conditioning →冷氣

available [əˈveləbl] →有得賣的；可得的

Unit 17
有關租車的資訊

 會話 1 **Dialogue 1**

 MP3 18

A Hello, Ace Rental.
喂,『一流租車公司』。

B Hi, I would like to rent a car for this weekend.
嗨,我這個週末想要租一部車。

I would like to know the prices for a 2-day rental.
我想知道租兩天的價格。

A We have a special on a midsize car.
我們有一型中型車正在特價優待。

It's $24.95 per day with unlimited miles.
它租一天是二十四元九毛五,不限里程。

B That sounds good.
那聽起來還可以。

What time can I pick it up on Friday?
我星期五幾點可以取車?

Ⓐ Any time after 2.

兩點以後隨時都行。

It will be due back on Saturday by 10.

星期六，十點以前要還車。

Ⓑ All right, I'll be in on Saturday.

好，我星期六會開回來。

會話
2 **Dialogue 2**

Ⓐ Hi, welcome to Al's Rent a Car.

嗨，你好，歡迎光臨『A1租車公司』。

Ⓑ I need a car for today.

我今天需要一部車。

Ⓐ What type of car would you like?

你想要什麼型式的車？

Ⓑ I need to save money.

我得省錢才行。

What is your best rate?

你們最低的租車費是多少？

Ⓐ We have a compact available for $19.95.

我們有一部現有的小型車，十九元九毛五一天。

Would you like to rent that one?

你要租那部嗎？

ⓑ That sounds like a good deal.
聽起來價格似乎不錯。

I'll take it.
我就要那部。

舉一反三 **Useful Sentences**

➲ 問租車的價格

01 How much is it to rent a mid-size car?
租一部中型車要多少錢？

02 What's the rate for a van?
小巴的租金多少？

03 What's the daily rate for a compact car?
一部小型車的每天租金是多少？

04 What's the weekly rate for a full-size car?
一部大型車的每星期租金是多少？

➲ 問其他的租車問題

01 Can I leave the car at another agency?
我可以在別的租車點還車嗎？

02 Can I leave the car in another state?
我可以開到別州還車嗎？

03 Can I return the car to an agency in another city?
我可以在別的都市的租車點還車嗎？

04 Is insurance included in the price?
這個價格包含保險金嗎？

重要英語單字 Vocabulary

rental [ˈrɛntl̩] →出租

price [praɪs] →價格

rate [ret] →價格；價碼

special [ˈspɛʃəl] →特價

unlimited [ʌnˈlɪmɪtɪd] →不限制的

van →多人座箱型車；小巴

compact car →小型轎車

midsize car →中型轎車

full-size car →大型轎車

agency [ˈedʒənsɪ] →代理商；辦事處

insurance [ɪnˈʃʊrəns] →保險

Unit 18

有關租公寓的資訊

Dialogue 1

Chapter 3

A Hello, I'm interested in renting an apartment.

喂，我有興趣要租一個公寓。

Do you have any apartments that rent for less than $300?

你們有沒有低於三百美元的公寓出租？

B We have one-bedroom apartments for $285 per month and two-bedroom apartments are just $325.

我們有單臥房的公寓，每月是兩百八十五美元，而雙臥房的才三百二十五美元而已。

A How big is the one-bedroom apartment?

單臥房的公寓有多大？

B It is about 700 square feet.

大概七百平方英尺左右。

It has a mini kitchen and one bathroom.

它有一個小廚房和一間浴室。

A Does it have much closet space?

它有很多櫥櫃的空間嗎？

B Actually, it has a lot of closet space.

事實上，它櫥櫃空間很多。

I think it is one of the best features of the apartment.

我想那是這型公寓最好的特點。

會話
2　**Dialogue 2**

A Hello, thank you for calling Greenland Apartment Center.

喂，謝謝你打電話來『格陵蘭公寓中心』。

How may I help you?

能為您服務嗎？

B I'm interested in a 2-bedroom apartment.

我有興趣想租一個雙臥房的公寓。

Do you have any available right now?

你們現在有現成的空房嗎？

A Yes, we have several to choose from.

有，我們有幾間可供選擇。

How soon do you need the apartment?

你多快需要這個公寓？

B I need to move in on the 15th.

我這個月十五號要搬入。

What are the rates on 2-bedroom apartments?

雙臥室公寓租金多少？

A They rent for $575 a month.

雙臥室公寓每個月租金五百七十五美元。

Would you like to stop by and take a look at the apartment?

你要不要到這裡來看看這個公寓？

B Sure, **I'll come by this afternoon.**

當然，我今天下午會來。

Thanks for your help.　Bye.

謝謝你的協助，再見。

Chapter 3

重要英語單字　Vocabulary

interested [ˈɪntrɪstɪd] →有興趣的

apartment [əˈpɑrtmənt] →公寓

square [skwɛr] →（數學）平方

mini →小的

kitchen [ˈkɪtʃən] →廚房

space [spes] →空間

feature [ˈfitʃɚ] →產品特點

stop by →順道拜訪

take a look →看看；瞧瞧

Unit 19

• • • • • • • • • •

有關機票的資訊

Dialogue 1

A Thank you for calling Japan Airlines.

謝謝您打電話來『日本航空公司』。

How may I help you?

能為您服務嗎？

B I need to know when flight 304 arrives from Hong Kong.

我要知道從香港起飛的第304班機何時會抵達？

A It lands at 5:16 at gate 18.

它五點十六分到，在第十八號登機門。

B What terminal is gate 18 in?

第十八號登機門在第幾航空站？

A It is in terminal 3.

它是在第三航空站。

B OK, thank you very much.

好，非常謝謝你。

會話 2 Dialogue 2

A I need to book a flight to Sidney today please.
我要訂一張今天到雪梨的機票。

How much is a one-way ticket?
單程票價多少？

B Would you like first class or coach?
你要頭等艙還是經濟艙？

A Coach please.
經濟艙。

B A one-way ticket in coach is $695.
經濟艙的單程票是六百九十五美元。

A How soon do the flights leave?
班機多快起飛？

B We have a flight leaving in one hour and another one in two and a half hours.
我們有一班一小時後起飛，還有另一班在兩個半鐘頭後離開。

舉一反三 Useful Sentences

➲ 問班機起降時間

01 When is flight 606 leaving?
六〇六班機幾點起飛？

02　Is flight 408 arriving on schedule?
四〇八班機會準時抵達嗎？

03　At which gate does flight 377 leave?
三七七班機在哪個登機門起飛？

04　At which gate does flight 377 arrive?
三七七班機在哪個登機門抵達？

重要英語單字　Vocabulary

airlines [ˈɛrˌlaɪnz] →航空公司

flight [flaɪt] →班機

gate [get] →登機門

terminal [ˈtɝmɪnḷ] →航空站

book a flight →買機票

one-way ticket →單程票

coach [kotʃ] →經濟艙

on schedule →準時

Unit 20
詢問有關旅行團的資訊

 會話 1 **Dialogue 1**

 MP3 21

A Hi, I'm interested in a tour package to the island.

嗨，我有興趣參加到這個島嶼的綜合旅行團。

What packages do you have?

你們有幾種綜合旅行團？

B We have two packages.

我們有兩種綜合旅行團。

We have a package for $135 that includes all transportation and food.

我們有一種一百三十五美元的，包括所有交通和餐飲。

The $55 package only covers your entrance fee to the island.

五十五美元的只涵蓋到島嶼的門票費。

A I think I prefer the first package.

我想我比較喜歡第一種綜合旅行團。

Do you accept credit cards?

你們收信用卡嗎？

B We sure do.

我們收。

Your total is $141.25 including tax.

含稅一共是一百四十一美元兩毛五。

Dialogue 2

Ⓐ Hi, do you have any tours in the Washington area?

嗨，你們在華盛頓地區有沒有旅行團？

Ⓑ Yes sir, we have three different tours.

先生，有的。我們有三種不同的旅行團。

One takes you to the White House.

一種帶你到白宮。

One shows you the downtown area.

一種帶你參觀市區。

And the third lets you explore the mall zone.

還有第三種讓你到大型購物中心去好好的考察考察。

Ⓐ How much is the White House tour?

到白宮的旅行團多少錢？

Ⓑ It's only $7.95 per person.

一個人只要七塊九毛五美元。

If you have more than 10 people, we can offer a group discount.

要是你們有十人以上，我們可以提供團體折扣。

Ⓐ I only need two tickets.

我只需要兩張票。

I would like to take that tour tomorrow afternoon.

我想參加明天下午的那個旅行團。

B OK, I just need your name to reserve your spots.

好，我只需要你的大名來幫你預留團位。

重要英語單字 Vocabulary

entrance ['ɛntrəns] →入門

entrance fee →進場費；門票

prefer [prɪ'fɝ] →較喜歡

accept [ək'sɛpt] →接受

credit cards →信用卡；信用咭

the White House →白宮；美國總統辦公室與住處

explore [ɪk'splor] →考察；探索

mall [mɔl] →大型購物中心

zone [zon] →規劃區

person ['pɝsn̩] →人

per person →每人

offer ['ɔfɚ] →提供

discount ['dɪskaʊnt] →折扣

group discount →團體折扣

afternoon [ˌæftɚ'nun] →下午

reserve [rɪ'zɝv] →預訂

spot [spɑt] →空位

Unit 21

有關入學的資訊

會話 1 Dialogue 1

MP3 22

Ⓐ Hi, **can I help you?**
嗨，有事嗎？

Ⓑ Yes, I need some information about applying to the school.
是的，我需要一些關於申請入學的資訊。

Ⓐ OK, here is an information packet.
好，這是一整套資料。

When are you interested in starting?
你打算什麼時候開始入學？

Ⓑ I'd like to begin this fall.
我想要從今年秋季班開始。

Do you have space for more students in the fall?
你們秋季班還有缺額可招更多學生嗎？

Ⓐ Yes, we do, but you need to apply quickly.
有，我們還有。但你要趕快申請。

Ⓑ All right, thanks for the information.
好，謝謝你提供的資訊。

會話 2 Dialogue 2

A Hi, I need some information about admission to the school.

嗨，我需要一些本校入學的資訊。

B What do you need?

你要知道什麼？

A I need to know the cost for tuition and the deadline for application.

我要知道學費多少以及申請的截止日期。

B Sure thing.

好。

Each semester hour is $80.

每個學期每學分八十美元。

You will have some fees in addition to that.

除此而外，你還會有一些費用。

The application must be turned in by the 15th of this month.

申請表必須在本月十五以前交。

A What are the other fees?

其他費用是什麼？

B They pay for use of the library and computer lab.

學生要付圖書館使用費和電腦實驗室費。

Good luck.

祝你好運。

重要英語單字　Vocabulary

information [ˌɪnfɚˈmeʃən] →資訊；訊息

apply [əˈplaɪ]申請

packet [ˈpækɪt] →資料袋

fall [fɔl] →（學校）秋季班；上學期

quickly [ˈkwɪklɪ] →快

admission [ədˈmɪʃən] →入學

tuition [tjuˈɪʃən] →學費

deadline [ˈdɛdˌlaɪn] →截止日期

application [ˌæpləˈkeʃən] →申請

semester [səˈmɛstɚ] →學期

in addition to~除了～之外

turn in →繳交

library [ˈlaɪbrɛrɪ] →圖書館

computer [kəmˈpjutɚ] →電腦

lab →實驗室；實驗課

Unit 22
用英語找工作

Chapter 3

Dialogue 1

A Hi, can I help you?
嗨，你好。有事可以為你服務嗎？

B Yes. **I would like an application.**
是的，我想要一份申請表。

A **OK, here you go.**
好的，在這兒。

Please fill it out completely.
請全部填寫。

We will also need a letter of recommendation.
我們還要求一封推薦函。

B Can I set up an interview for tomorrow?
我可以約在明天面談嗎？

A Sure. How's 3:00?
當然，三點怎麼樣？

B That will be great.
那好極了。

I'll have the application and letter tomorrow when I come in.
明天我來的時候，會帶申請表和推薦信來。

89

會話 2 Dialogue 2

Ⓐ Hi, do you have any positions open right now?

嗨，你們現在有沒有職位開缺？

Ⓑ Yes, we are taking applications for all positions.

有，我們所有的職位現在都正在接受申請中。

Ⓐ I'm interested in a part time job as a cashier.

我有興趣做兼職的收銀員。

Ⓑ OK, just fill out this application and bring it back by tomorrow.

好，只要把這份申請表填一填，明天拿回來。

Ⓐ Would it be OK to fill it out now?

現在填寫可以嗎？

Ⓑ Sure, that would be fine.

當然，那也沒問題。

重要英語單字 Vocabulary

fill out →（表格）填寫

completely [kəmˈplitlɪ] →完全地

recommendation [ˌrɛkəmənˈdeʃən] →推薦

letter of recommendation →推薦信

set up →訂定

interview [ˈɪntəˌvju] →面談

position [pəzɪʃən] →職位

open [ˈopən] →出缺的

right now →現在;此刻

part time →兼職的

job [dʒɑb] →職務

cashier [kæˈʃɪr] →收銀員;結帳員

Chapter 3

每天開口說一句

Chapter

4

問路英語

問路

會話 1 　Dialogue 1

A Excuse me, do you know how to get to the library?

對不起，你知道去圖書館該怎麼走法？

B Yes. Do you see that building ahead?

知道。你看見前面那棟建築嗎？

A Yes, I do.

有，我看見了。

B Well, go past it and you will see the library on the right.

那，走過它，你就會看見圖書館在你的右邊。

A OK. Thanks for your help.

好，謝謝你的幫忙。

B You're welcome.

不用客氣。

會話 2 　Dialogue 2

A May I help you?

有事嗎？

🅑 Yes. Could you tell me how to get to the student union?

是的。可否請你告訴我到學生活動中心怎麼走？

🅐 You bet. Enter the campus from University Drive and turn left on the second intersection.

沒問題。你從大學路進校園，在第二個十字路口左轉。

The student union is in the first building on your right.

學生活動中心就在你右邊第一棟建築裡面。

🅑 Can I enter from the opposite side of the campus?

我可以從校園的後邊哪裡進來嗎？

🅐 No, all of the streets on that side are under construction.

不行，那邊所有的街道都在施工中。

🅑 All right, thanks for your help.

好的，謝謝你的協助。

Chapter 4

30秒破解英語會話

　　出門在外，總會有需要問路的時候，若是需要用英語問路時，只要記住幾個基本句型就行，我們以圖書館來做例子，要問如何到圖書館，也就是要問：the way to the library（到圖書館的路），how to get to the library（如何到圖書館）以及where is the library（圖書館在哪裡）；至於如何問，英語會話裡有：Could you tell me ～?Can you tell me～?以及Do you know～?等三種問法，

例如：Could you tell me the way to the library?

　以下實用例句中的「指路」例句，是一個指路到圖書館的例子，這個完整的例子已包含了所有指路可能用到的英語句子，例如：那裡有個紅綠燈(There's a light.)，遇到南京路時右轉(Turn right on Nan-King Road)，你會看到圖書館在你的左邊(You'll see the library on your left.)等等。

舉一反三 **Useful Sentences**

● 問路

01	Could you tell me the way to the library? 你可不可以告訴我到圖書館的路怎麼走？
02	Could you please tell me how to get to the library? 可否請你告訴我要怎麼走到圖書館？
03	Could you tell me where the nearest restroom is? 妳能不能告訴我離這裡最近的洗手間在哪裡？
04	Can you tell me where the restroom is? 你能告訴我洗手間在哪裡嗎？
05	Do you know where the restroom is? 你知道洗手間在哪裡嗎？

● 其他問法

01	How do you get to the store? 到商店該如何走法？

02 Explain the directions, please.
請解釋一下方向。

03 What street is the store on?
商店在哪條街啊？

04 Where is McDonald's?
『麥當勞』在哪裡？

05 Is this the way to the station?
這是到火車站的路嗎？

➲ 指路

01 Go straight ahead here until you come to a big intersection.
從這裡直走，一直走到一個大十字路口為止。

02 That's First Street.
那就是第一街。

03 There's a light there.
那兒有個紅綠燈。

04 Take a left at the light on First Street.
在第一街的紅綠燈左轉。

05 Go about half a kilometer.
向前走大約半公里。

06 And then there's a kind of Y in the road.
然後，那裡有個類似三岔路的地方。

07 So you have to keep to the right.
所以你必須保持在右邊。

Chapter 4

08 **After that, take the first left you come to.**
過了那以後，你在第一個能轉彎的地方左轉。

09 **That will be Main Street, which takes you to Forest Road.**
那就是緬因街，從緬因街你就可以到森林路。

10 **There's a stop sign there.**
那裡有個『停』的標誌。

11 **That's where the McDonald's is.**
『麥當勞』就在那裡。

12 **You can't miss it.**
你不會錯過的。

13 **Turn right on Forest Road.**
在森林路右轉。

重要英語單字 Vocabulary

light [laɪt] →交通燈；紅綠燈

building [ˈbɪldɪŋ] →大樓；建築物

past [pæst] →經過

student union →學生活動中心

construction [kənˈstrʌkʃən] →建造

nearest [ˈnɪrɪst] →最靠近的

directions [dəˈrɛkʃənz] →方向

intersection [ˌɪntəˈsɛkʃən] →十字路口

straight [stret] →直直地

Unit 24

問如何到某個觀光地

會話 1 — **Dialogue 1**

🄐 Hi, can you tell me where Texas Stadium is?
嗨，可以請你告訴我『德州體育館』在哪裡嗎？

🄑 Sure, it's in Dallas on First Street.
當然可以，它是在達拉斯的第一街上。

🄐 How do I get there from Fort Worth?
我從渥斯堡去那裡該怎麼走法？

🄑 Take I-30 east.
走I-30號公路。

Exit on First Street and go north.
在第一街出口下公路，往北走。

The stadium will be on your right.
體育館會在你的右方。

🄐 How long will I be on First Street?
我在第一街上還要開多久？

🄑 About 10 minutes, depending upon traffic.
大約十分鐘吧，要看交通狀況而定。

Chapter 4

會話 2 **Dialogue 2**

Ⓐ Can you tell me how to get to the museum?

可以請你告訴我到博物館該怎麼走嗎？

Ⓑ Where will you be coming from?

你要從哪裡過來？

Ⓐ From Arlington.

從阿靈頓市過來。

Ⓑ Sure, take I-30 west.

是這樣啊，你上西向I-三十號公路。

Exit when you see the sign for the museum.

當你看見博物館的牌誌時，就下公路。

Turn right and you'll be there in about 2 minutes.

向右轉，大約兩分鐘你就到了。

Ⓐ OK, do I need to pay for parking?

好，我懂。我停車得付錢嗎？

Ⓑ No, parking is free.

不用，停車是免費的。

舉一
反三 **Useful Sentences**

➲ 問到某個地方怎麼走

01 Can you tell me where Central Stadium is?
你可不可以告訴我『中央體育館』在哪裡？

02 Can you tell me how to get to the museum?
妳能不能跟我講怎樣去博物館？

03 Could you tell me the way to the Central Park?
你能不能告訴我到『中央公園』的路怎麼走？

重要英語單字 Vocabulary

stadium [ˈstedɪəm] →體育館

exit →出口；下高速公路

north [nɔrθ] →北方

depending upon~視～情況而定

traffic [ˈtræfɪk] →交通狀況

museum [mjuˈzɪəm] →博物館

sign →號誌；牌子

turn →轉

parking [ˈpɑrkɪŋ] →停車；泊車

Chapter 4

Unit 25

問如何到對方的住所

（注意住址的讀法，聽MP3）

會話 1 **Dialogue 1**

Ⓐ Mary, can you tell me how to get to your house?

瑪莉，可否請你告訴我到妳家該怎麼走法？

Ⓑ Sure.　Take Main street east all the way to First Street.

沒問題。你走緬因街向東，一直走到第一街。

Turn right on First Street and go to 1543 First Street.

在第一街右轉，到第一街一千五百四十三號。

Ⓐ Is your house on the right or left?

妳家是在左邊還是右邊？

Ⓑ It's on the right.

在右邊。

It's the only two-story house on the right.

是右邊唯一的一棟兩層樓。

Ⓐ OK, I'll be there around 8. Bye.

好，我大約八點左右會到。再見。

Ⓑ See you later.

再見。

會話 2 Dialogue 2

A Mary, do you want to come over tomorrow?

瑪莉，妳明天要不要到我家來？

B Yes, but I don't know how to get to your house.

要啊，可是我不知道到你家要怎麼走。

A Oh, that's right.

噢，對呀。

Do you have a pen handy?

妳手邊有沒有筆？

B Yep, go ahead.

有，你講吧。

A OK, go down First Street to the end of the road and turn right.

好，沿第一街直走，到路底右轉。

It's the second house on your left.

就在妳左方的第二棟房子。

It's easy to find.

很容易找的。

B That sounds easy.

聽起來是很容易。

I'll see you tomorrow.

那就明天見了。

舉一反三　**Useful Sentences**

● 問到對方住所的路

01 Please tell me directions to your house.
請告訴我到你家的方位。

02 Can you tell me how to get to your house?
你可以告訴我怎樣到你家嗎？

03 I don't know how to get to your house.
我不知道到你家該怎麼走。

重要英語單字　Vocabulary

story ['storɪ] →（樓房）樓層

around →大約

later ['letɚ] →稍後

come over →到我家來

right →對

handy ['hændɪ] →方便的；就在手邊的

Yep [jɛp] →是（Yes的口語說法）

go ahead →儘管做吧

road [rod] →路

second ['sɛkənd] →第二的

Chapter

5

互助英語

Unit 26

請求幫忙

Dialogue 1

🅐 Help! I'm trapped.

來人幫忙啊，我被困住了！

🅑 Where are you?

妳在哪兒呀？

🅐 I'm in the closet.

我在衣間裡。

The door shut on me.

門自己關上，把我關在裡面了。

🅑 OK, stay calm.

好了，別緊張，保持冷靜。

I'll get you out.

我會把妳弄出來。

🅐 Just get the keys off of the desk and open the door.

你只要到桌上去拿鑰匙，開門就行了。

🅑 All right, I've got them.

好了，好了，我拿到了。

There you go.

喏，開了。

Everything is fine.

萬事平安。

會話
2
Dialogue 2

Ⓐ Sam, would you help me carry these boxes?

山姆，幫我拿這些盒子好嗎？

Ⓑ Sure. Which ones?

當然，哪幾個？

Ⓐ Take the big box.

拿這個大盒子。

I'll get these 3 little ones.

我會拿這三個小的。

Ⓑ OK, then I'll get the other big box.

好，過後我再拿剩下的一個大的。

Ⓐ Great, thanks for your help!

太好了，謝謝你的幫忙。

Ⓑ Any time.

不客氣。

I'm glad to help.

我很樂意幫忙的。

Chapter 5

舉一反三 **Useful Sentences**

➔ 請求幫忙

01 Help!
來人幫幫忙啊！

02 Could you help me with this?
你能幫我作這個嗎？

03 Could you give me a hand?
你能幫我一下忙嗎？

04 Can you carry this for me?
你能幫我拿這個嗎？

05 Would you hold the door please?
請你幫我把門扶著，別讓它關上。

➔ 有人要求幫忙時，你怎麼說

01 Sure, I'll help you.
當然，我會幫你的。

02 OK.
沒問題！

04 Yes, I'll give you a hand.
好，我來幫你一個忙。

05 What's wrong?
怎麼了？

06 There you go.
好了。

重要英語單字 Vocabulary

trapped [træp] →遭困住（trap的過去分詞）

closet [ˈklɑzɪt] →衣櫥；衣間

shut →關

calm →冷靜

key →鑰匙

carry [ˈkærɪ] →攜帶

little [ˈlɪtl̩] →小的

glad →樂意

每天開口說一句

請人家喝飲料

Dialogue 1

Ⓐ **Would you like something to drink?**
你要不要喝點東西？

Ⓑ **Sure, what do you have?**
好啊，你有什麼？

Ⓐ **We have Coke, 7 Up, and tea.**
我們有可口可樂、七喜汽水、還有茶。

Ⓑ **I would like a Coke.**
我要可樂。

Ⓐ **What size?**
多大杯？

Ⓑ **A large, please.**
請給我大杯的。

會話 2 **Dialogue 2**

Ⓐ **Could I get you a drink?**
你要喝杯飲料嗎？

Ⓑ **Please. That would be great.**
那很好，請給我弄一杯。

A How about some water?

來點水怎麼樣？

B OK. Do you have lemons?

好，你有沒有檸檬？

A Yes, how many would you like?

好，你要幾片？

B Three, please.

三片。

Thanks a lot.

謝謝。

舉一
反三　**Useful Sentences**

➲ 問來客是否要喝飲料，怎麼說

01	Can I get you anything to drink? 你要喝些什麼飲料嗎？
02	Would you care for coffee? 你要不要喝咖啡？
03	Would you care for coffee or tea? 你要喝咖啡還是茶？
04	Would you like a drink? 你要喝點飲料？

Chapter 5

➲ **有人問你是否要喝飲料，你怎麼回答**

01 Sure, I'll take a coke.
好，我要可樂。

02 Sure, what do you have?
好，你有些什麼？

重要英語單字 Vocabulary

size [saɪz] →大小；尺碼

get [gɛt] →拿

get a drink →拿飲料

great [gret] →很好

lemon [lɛmən] →檸檬

care for →（口語）要不要

like [laɪk] →喜歡

Unit 28
· · · · · · · · · ·
出借東西

會話
1 ▶ **Dialogue 1**

MP3 29

🅐 **Sam, would you like to borrow my hammer?**
山姆，要不要借我的釘鎚？

🅑 **If you don't mind.**
好啊，要是你不介意的話。

🅐 **Of course not.**
當然不介意。

🅑 **OK, I'll return it tomorrow.**
好，我明天會還你。

🅐 That's fine, but **just keep it as long as you need it.**
好，不過你要用多久儘管留著用。

🅑 **Thanks a lot.**
非常謝謝。

You're a great help.
你幫了我一個大忙。

Chapter 5

會話
2
Dialogue 2

🅐 Hi, what are you doing?
你好啊，你在幹嘛？

🅑 I'm trying to paint this cabinet, but my brush isn't working well.
我試著要給這個櫃子上漆，不過我的刷子不怎麼好用。

🅐 Would you like to borrow mine?
你要不要借我的？

🅑 Sure, that would be wonderful.
當然，那太好了。

🅐 I'll go get it for you.
我去拿來給你。

🅑 OK, thanks.
好，謝了。

舉一
反三
Useful Sentences

⊃ 提出願意幫忙對方

01　Do you want to borrow my tools?
你要不要借我的工具？

02　Would you like to borrow mine?
你要不要借我的去用？

03　I could lend you $100, if you'd like.
如果你要的話，我可以借你一百美元。

➔ 有人提出要幫你忙時，你怎麼回答

01
Sure, that would be great!
當然了，那太好了。

02
OK.
好啊！

03
No, thanks. I've got it.
謝謝，不用了。我自己有。

04
Thanks a lot.
多謝。

05
OK, I appreciate it.
好啊，謝謝你。

重要英語單字　Vocabulary

borrow ['bɑro] →借

hammer ['hæmɚ] →釘鎚；槌子

mind [maɪnd] →介意

of course →當然

return [rɪ'tɝn] →歸還

keep [kip] →保留

paint [pent] →油漆

cabinet ['kæbənɛt] →櫃子

brush [brʌʃ] →刷子

working well →工作正常；好用

appreciate [ə'priʃɪ͵et] →感激

Chapter 5

會話 1　Dialogue 1

ⓐ Jane, where are you going?

珍恩，妳上哪去啊？

ⓑ To the student center.

到學生活動中心。

ⓐ **Would you like a ride?**

要不要我載妳去？

I'm going right by there.

我正好會經過那裡。

ⓑ Yes.　You're very kind.

好啊。你這個人真好。

ⓐ Any time you need a ride, just let me know.

妳隨時需要人載的話，就通知我。

ⓑ Thanks a lot.

多謝了。

會話 2　Dialogue 2

ⓐ Amy, would you like to borrow my car for your trip?

艾美啊，妳這趟出門要不要借我的車？

Ⓑ Oh, I don't know.
嗯……不知道耶。

I'd feel scared that I might wreck it.
人家好怕把車子給撞壞了。

Ⓐ You won't wreck it.
妳不會撞車的。

I trust you.
我信得過妳。

Ⓑ Well, if it's OK with you.
那，要是你那邊沒問題的話……

Ⓐ Sure, I'll even fill it up with gas for you.
當然沒問題。我甚至還會幫你把油加滿。

Ⓑ Wow, you're a good friend. Thanks a lot.
哇，你這個朋友真夠意思。多謝了。！

舉一反三 **Useful Sentences**

⊃ 有意讓人搭便車的說法

01 **Do you need a ride?**
你需要人用車送你一程嗎？

02 **Would you like a ride?**
你要搭便車嗎？

重要英語單字　Vocabulary

ride [raɪd] →搭載

kind [kaɪnd] →良善；好心

trip [trɪp] →旅程；出門一遊

scared [skɛrd] →害怕

wreck [rɛk] →撞車

fill up →加滿（汽油等）

friend [frɛnd] →朋友

每天開口說一句

社交英語

請客

（用餐完畢，結帳時……）

Ⓐ How much do I owe you?
我應給你多少錢？

Ⓑ I've got it.
我都付了。

This one's on me.
這一頓我請客。

Ⓐ You don't need to do that.
你不用這麼做的。

Ⓑ I want to.
我要做。

I haven't paid for your dinner in a while.
我好久沒幫你付過吃飯的錢了。

Ⓐ Well, thanks a lot.
那，非常謝謝了。

Ⓑ You bet.
不客氣。

It's my pleasure.

我的榮幸。

會話 2 **Dialogue 2**

A Here's 300 Yuan for my ticket.

這裡是我的票錢三百元，

B Keep it.

收著吧。

I'm buying tonight.

今晚我付錢。

A No, you can't do that.

不行呀，你不可以這樣。

B Sure I can.

我當然可以這樣。

My treat.

我請客。

A All right, but I'm buying next time.

好吧，不過下回我付錢。

B It's a deal.

一言為定。

30秒破解英語會話

　　buy這個字原本的意思是「付錢買東西」，所以要請客，也就是替對方付錢買東西的意思，例如：你要請對方喝飲料，英語的說法就是Let me buy you a drink.或者你要說「今晚我請客」，英語的說法就是I'm buying tonight.

舉一
反三　　**Useful Sentences**

⊃ 我請客，怎麼說

01　I'll get that.
　　我來付錢。

02　My treat.
　　我請客。

03　This one's on me.
　　這一份我請客了。

04　I'll pay for this.
　　我來付這個錢。

05　I'm treating tonight.
　　今晚我請客。

06　I'm buying tonight.
　　今晚我付錢。

07　Let me buy you a drink.
　　讓我請你喝杯酒。

● 有人要請客時，你怎麼回答

01 You don't have to do that.
你不用這麼做的。

02 OK, but let me pay next time.
好，不過下回讓我付錢。

03 Thanks, I appreciate it.
謝了，我很感激。

04 Wow, you're very kind.
哇，你做人真好。

05 No, let me pay.
不，讓我來付！

重要英語單字 Vocabulary

owe [o] →虧欠

on me →（口語）我請客

dinner [ˈdɪnɚ] →晚餐；正餐

in a while →好久

Yuan [juˈɑn] →元（台灣貨幣單位）

deal →交易

Chapter 6

Unit 31

敬酒

Dialogue 1

🅐 Excuse me, **can I have everyone's attention, please?**

對不起，請大家聽我說。

🅑 Sam, what are you doing?

山姆，你在幹嘛？

🅐 **You'll see.**

你馬上會明白。

（對眾人……）

I'd like to propose a toast to our new secretary.

我想要大家為我們的新秘書敬一杯酒。

Mary, welcome on board.

瑪莉，歡迎加入我們！

🅑 Thanks, Sam. You really go out of the way to make me feel welcome. Thanks a lot.

山姆，謝謝你。你真是煞費心思來讓我感到受歡迎。非常感謝你。

🅐 Three cheers for Mary.

給瑪莉三聲歡呼！

C Hip hip hooray!

嘿！嘿！嘿！

會話 2 **Dialogue 2**

A May I have your attention, please?

請大家聽我說。

I have an announcement to make.

我要作一項宣佈。

Would Mary Ann please come forward?

有請瑪莉安到前面來。

B Here I am.

我在這兒！

A **Come forward.**

到前面來。

I'd like to propose a toast to my wife Mary Ann, Teacher of the Year.

我要請大家為我太太瑪莉安敬一杯酒，她獲選『年度最佳教師』。

C Hooray! Way to go Mary Ann!

嘿！再接再厲，瑪莉安！

A Mary Ann worked hard all year.

瑪莉安一年到頭辛勤工作。

She really deserved the honor.

她得到這份榮譽是實至名歸。

Chapter 6

> I just want to say that I'm proud to be her husband.
>
> 我只要說，我身為她的丈夫很感驕傲。

B Thank you everyone. Thank you very much.
謝謝大家，非常謝謝你們！

舉一
反三 **Useful Sentences**

➲ 要大家敬酒的說法

01 I'd like to propose a toast.
我要提議敬一杯酒。

02 Three cheers for David.
為大衛歡呼三聲！

03 Here's to you.
敬你！

04 To our favorite friend.
敬我們最喜愛的朋友！

05 This is a toast for John.
這杯酒是敬約翰的！

➲ 30秒學會祝酒

01 Hooray!
嘿！

02 Cheers.
大家乾哪！

(Clap.)
（拍手鼓掌）

03 (singing) For he's a jolly good fellow, for he's a jolly good fellow, for he's a jolly good fellow, and nobody can deny.

（唱歌）他真是個好人、他真是個好人、他真是個好人，誰都不容否認。

04 Hail to the chief.
給老闆歡呼！

重要英語單字　Vocabulary

attention [əˈtɛnʃən] →注意

propose [prəˈpoz] →提議

secretary [ˈsɛkrəˌtɛrɪ] →秘書

cheers [tʃɪrz] →歡呼

announcement [əˈnaʊnsmənt] →宣佈

toast [tost] →祝酒

husband [ˈhʌzbənd] →丈夫

favorite [ˈfevərɪt] →最喜愛的

Hooray! [hʊˈre] →嘿！（歡呼聲）

hail [hel] →歡呼

Chapter 7

徵詢英語

Unit 32
請求同意

Dialogue 1

（放學要先到同學家……）

A Can I go to Scott's house?
我可以上史考特的家嗎？

B How long will you be gone?
你要去多久？

A Until 7.
到七點。

His mom said she would bring me back.
他媽媽說她會帶我回家。

B OK, as long as you call me when you get there.
好，只要你到他家的時候給我打電話就行。

A All right, I will. Bye.
好，我會的。再見。

B Bye, I love you.
再見，我疼你！

Dialogue 2

A Can I ask a favor?
我可以請求你同意一件事嗎？

B Sure, go ahead.

可以，講吧。

A Would it be all right if I went to Los Angels next weekend?

我下週末到洛杉磯可以嗎？

B What for?

為什麼呢？

A Well, I want to surprise John by showing up for his birthday.

喔，我要在約翰的生日上現身，讓他驚奇一下。

B Well, that sounds like it would be OK.

是麼，那聽起來好像還可以答應。

Just be careful.

只是要小心一點。

舉一反三 **Useful Sentences**

⊃ 請求對方的同意

01
Can I go to Mary's house?
我可以上瑪莉家嗎？

02
Is it all right if I go to a movie?
我去看場電影可以嗎？

03
Is it OK to eat in here?
在這裡吃東西，行嗎？

04
May I go to John's?
我可以到約翰家嗎？

⊃ 同意對方的要求

01 OK, but be back by 9:00.
可以，但九點前要回家。

02 Sure, have fun.
當然，好好地玩吧！

03 You bet.
沒問題。

⊃ 不同意對方的要求

01 No, not tonight.
不，今晚不行。

02 No, you'd better not.
不行，你最好不要。

重要英語單字　Vocabulary

as long as →只要
call →打電話
favor [ˈfevɚ] →同意；支持
all right →好
surprise [səˈpraɪz] →驚奇
show up →出現；現身
careful [ˈkɛrfəl] →小心
John's →（單獨一個字出現）約翰的家
had better →最好（實際上經常說成'd better）

徵詢對方意見

會話 1 — Dialogue 1

MP3 34

Ⓐ John, do you like the opera?
約翰，你喜歡歌劇嗎？

Ⓑ No, not really.
不，不怎麼喜歡。

Ⓐ Why is that?
那又為什麼？

Ⓑ Well, it's very expensive and they're usually singing in another language.
噢，那很貴，而且歌劇一般都是用別的語言唱的。

That kind of gets on my nerves.
那有點讓我心裡發毛。

Ⓐ Yah, **that makes sense.**
是啊，說的倒也是。

But you should at least go once.
不過你最少也得去看一回。

You might like it.
也許你會喜歡的。

會話 2 Dialogue 2

Ⓐ Hey, can I ask a favor?
喂，能不能幫我個小忙？

Ⓑ Sure, what do you need?
可以呀，你需要什麼？

Ⓐ Tell me whether you like the blue skirt or the jeans better.
告訴我你比較喜歡這件藍裙還是這條牛仔褲。

Ⓑ OK, hold them up.
好，把它們舉高一點。

Hmm, I think I like the jeans better.
嗯，我想我比較喜歡牛仔褲。

Ⓐ You do? Do you think they go with this shirt?
真的嗎？依你看，這件牛仔褲跟這件襯衫配嗎？

Ⓑ Yes, I think that looks good.
配，我想那樣看起來很好看。

舉一反三 Useful Sentences

⊃ 請問對方的意見

01	Do you like this? 你喜歡這個嗎？
02	What do you think about my dress? 你認為我的洋裝怎麼樣？

03 Do you like blue or green better?
你較喜歡藍色還是綠色？

04 How do you feel about that?
你對那件事的感覺如何？

05 What's your opinion?
你有什麼看法？

➲ 當有人問你的意見時

01 I like that a lot.
我滿喜歡那個。

02 That's really great!
那真好。

03 I don't like it that much.
我不是挺喜歡的。

04 It's OK.
還好啦。

05 I'm not sure.
我不知道耶。

06 I don't know.
我不知道。

重要英語單字　Vocabulary

opera [ˈɑpərə] →歌劇

expensive [ɪkˈspɛnsɪv] →昂貴

language [ˈlæŋgwɪdʒ] →語言

kind of →有一點

gets on my nerves →叫人覺得不自在

make sense →有道理

favor [ˈfevɚ] →幫忙

skirt [skɝt] →裙子

jeans [dʒinz] →牛仔褲

hold [hold] →用手舉著

每天開口說一句

Ⓐ **Ma'am, could I have a coke please?**
小姐，請給我一杯可樂。

Ⓑ **Sure. Would you like ice?**
好。你要冰嗎？

Ⓐ **Yes, please. Could you also bring some napkins?**
要，請給我冰。可否請妳也帶一些餐巾來？

Ⓑ **I'd be happy to.**
我很樂意幫你拿。

Ⓐ **Thanks a lot.**
多謝。

Ⓑ **Yes, sir.**
好的，先生。

會話 **2**   **Dialogue 2**

Ⓐ **Yes sir, what can I get you?**
先生，要我給你拿什麼？

Ⓑ **Is there a meal on the flight?**
這班飛機有沒有餐點？

Ⓐ No sir, I'm sorry there's not.
先生，沒有耶。很抱歉，沒有。

Ⓑ Could I have some peanuts then, please?
那，能否請給我一些花生豆？

Ⓐ Sure.　Would you like a drink?
可以。你要飲料嗎？

Ⓑ Yes, please.　**I'll take a Coke.**
要，請幫我倒。我要可樂。

舉一反三　**Useful Sentences**

⊃ **在飛機上，如何向空中小姐要東西**

01　Could I have a coke?
我可以要一杯可樂嗎？

02　I'd like a hamburger.
我想要一個漢堡。

03　May we have some napkins, please?
我們可不可以要一些餐巾？

04　Could you bring us some more water?
妳能幫我們再拿一些水來嗎？

⊃ **空中小姐的回答**

01　Sure.
沒問題。

02 OK, I'll have that right out.
好，我馬上端出來。

03 Can I get you anything else?
你還要什麼其他的東西嗎？

04 Yes, sir, I'll get that for you.
好的，先生，我幫你去拿。

重要英語單字　Vocabulary

ice [aɪs] →冰

napkins [ˈnæpkɪnz] →餐巾

happy [ˈhæpɪ] →快樂

meal [mil] →餐點

peanut [ˈpinət] →落花生

hamburger [ˈhæm͵bɝɡɚ] →漢堡

right [raɪt] →馬上

anything else →其他的東西

Unit 35
· · · · · · · · · ·
在飯店

會話 1 　Dialogue 1

A Hello, Room Service.　Can I help you?
喂，客房服務。可以為您服務嗎？

B Yes, **I'd like to have dinner delivered to my room.**
是的，我想要訂晚餐，送到我房間來。

A Yes, sir.　Which room are you in?
好的，先生。你在哪號房？

B 225.
二二五號。

A OK, what would you like?
好，你要點什麼？

B I want a hamburger and a pitcher of water.
我要一份漢堡和一大罐水。

會話 2 　Dialogue 2

A Hi, could you tell me where the hotel pool is?
嗨，可否請妳告訴我飯店的游泳池在哪裡？

B Yes, it's on the first floor next to the gym.
可以，它是在一樓健身房隔壁。

Here's a map.

這是地圖。

A Do they have towels at the pool?

游泳池那裡有沒有浴巾？

B Yes, just give them your room number.

有，只要把你的房間號碼跟他們講就行。

A OK, thanks for your help.

好，謝謝你的幫忙。

B You're welcome, sir.

先生，不客氣。

重要英語單字 Vocabulary

service ['sɝvɪs] →服務

delivered [dɪ'lɪvɚd] →送貨（deliver的過去分詞）

pitcher ['pɪtʃɚ] →（裝飲料的）大罐子

pool [pul] →游泳池

gym [dʒɪm] →健身房

map [mæp] →地圖

Unit 36

用餐時

Dialogue 1

（在餐館……）

Ⓐ **May we have some more rolls, please?**
我們能否再跟你要些小麵包？

Ⓑ Sure. How many would you like?
行。你們要幾個？

Ⓐ Three. **We also need some more butter.**
三個。我們也要再一些奶油。

Ⓑ OK. Can I bring you anything else?
好。還有別的東西可以給您送來嗎？

Ⓐ No, thanks.
沒有了，謝謝。

Ⓑ I'll have the rolls right out.
我馬上把小麵包拿來。

Dialogue 2

（在朋友家中……）

Ⓐ Excuse me, Diana.
對不起，戴安娜。

B Yes, what can I do for you?

嗄，要我做什麼嗎？

A I'd like another drink.

我想要再來一杯飲料。

B Are you drinking Coke?

你喝的是可口可樂嗎？

A Yes, but I actually want some water now.

是，不過事實上我現在想要一點水。

B OK, I'll get it for you.

好，我幫你去拿。

舉一
反三　**Useful Sentences**

⊃ 在餐廳，如何向服務生要東西

01　Could I have a coke?

請給我一杯可樂。

02　I'd like a hamburger.

我要一份漢堡。

03　May we have chopsticks, please?

可以給我們筷子嗎？

04　Could you bring us some more water?

請你再給我們一些水。

Chapter 8

⊃ 服務生的回答

01 Sure.
當然。

02 OK, I'll have that right out.
好,我馬上拿來。

03 Can I get you anything else?
還要什麼別的東西嗎?

04 Yes, sir, I'll get that for you.
好的,先生。我幫你去拿。

重要英語單字 Vocabulary

chopsticks [ˈtʃɑpˌstɪks] →筷子
actually [ˈæktʃʊəlɪ] →實際上

辦公室裡

會話 1 Dialogue 1

🅐 Cindy, would you copy this report for me?
辛蒂，請妳幫我影印這份報告好嗎？

🅑 Yes, sir. Are there any special requirements?
是，先生。有沒有特別要求要注意呢？

🅐 Yes. I need the report copied on transparency paper.
有，我要的是把這份報告影印在投影片上。

🅑 Is that all?
就是這樣嗎？

🅐 Yes, that is it. Thank you, Cindy.
是的，就是這樣。謝謝你，辛蒂。

🅑 You're welcome.
不客氣。

會話 2 Dialogue 2

🅐 John, would you pass me the stapler, please?
約翰，請你把訂書機遞給我。

🅑 Sure, here it is.
好，在這裡。

Ⓐ Thanks.

謝謝。

All right, that does it.   All finished.

好，這就好了。全完成了。

Here you go.

給你。

Ⓑ Thanks.   Could I file the report for you?

謝謝。要我幫你把報告歸檔嗎？

Ⓐ Yes, but I need to make a copy first.

好，不過，我得先做一份影印。

Ⓑ I can do that for you.

我可以幫你做。

重要英語單字   Vocabulary

copy [ˈkɑpɪ] →影印

report [rɪˈport] →報告

special [ˈspɛʃəl] →特別的

requirements [rɪˈkwaɪrmənts] →特定的要求

transparency [trænsˈpærənsɪ] →（簡報用）投影片

stapler [ˈsteplɚ] →訂書機

finished [ˈfɪnɪʃt] →做完了

英語會話詢問篇

請推薦可靠的人

Ⓐ Mary, do you know of a good doctor in the area?

瑪莉，妳知道這附近有哪位好一點的醫生嗎？

Ⓑ Well, the doctor we go to is pretty good.

嗯，我們看的醫生相當不錯。

Ⓐ What's his name?

他叫什麼名字？

Ⓑ He's Dr. Lee.

他是李醫師

His office is on the corner of 5th.

他的診所在第五街轉角處。

Ⓐ Do you have his number?

妳有他的電話號碼嗎？

Ⓑ It's 276-5656.

電話是276-5656。

He can probably get you in tomorrow.

他可能可以讓你明天去看他。

會話 2 Dialogue 2

A John, you know of any mechanics in the area?
約翰，你知道這附近有哪一位修車技師嗎？

B There are three in town, but I wouldn't recommend any of them.
鎮上有三個，但是我不會推薦他們當中任何一個。

A Oh really?
喔，真的嗎？

B Yah, they all seem to take too long.
是的，他們修車似乎都要修很久。

There is a good mechanic in Dallas though.
但是，達拉斯有一個好的修車技師。

A What is his name?
他叫什麼名字？

B His name is Robert Lin.
他叫林羅伯。

I'll give you his number.
我會給你他的電話號碼。

舉一
反三　**Useful Sentences**

● 請推薦可靠的人

01 Do you know of any mechanics in the area?
你知道這附近有哪位修車技師嗎？

02 Do you know of a good doctor?
你知道這附近有哪位好一點的醫生嗎？

03 Where do you go to the doctor?
你去哪裡看醫生？

04 Who should I see about this?
這個問題我應該找誰？

● 給人推介的說法

01 I like Dr. Lin. He works in Dallas.
我喜歡林醫師，他在達拉斯上班。

02 You should check with Dr. Lee.
你應該與李醫師談一談。

重要英語單字　Vocabulary

corner [ˈkɔrnɚ] →角落

recommend [ˌrɛkəˈmɛnd] →介紹

mechanic [məˈkænɪk] →修車的技師

area →地區

Unit 39
請介紹好玩的地方

會話 1 ▶ Dialogue 1

Ⓐ Where's a good place to eat around here?
這附近有什麼地方可以吃到好吃的？

Ⓑ What kind of food are you hungry for?
你想吃什麼？

Ⓐ I'm in the mood for pizza.
我好想吃匹薩餅。

Ⓑ There's a pizza place on the corner of Avenue K.
在K街轉角處有一家賣匹薩餅的店。

It's pretty good.
東西做得很好。

Ⓐ Is it expensive?
很貴嗎？

Ⓑ No, the prices are pretty reasonable.
不會，價錢很合理。

會話 2 Dialogue 2

A Hey John, you know of a good hotel in Dallas?

嗨，約翰，達拉斯附近你知道有哪一家旅館較好嗎？

B Sure, there are tons of good hotels in Dallas.

有，達拉斯有很多家好的旅館。

Which part of Dallas?

你要達拉斯的哪一區？

A Close to the airport.

靠近機場。

B The Holiday Inn is in the airport.

假日旅館就在機場內。

A How much is a room there?

哪裡的房間一間多少錢？

B About $1000 per night.

每晚大約一千元。

You should call them.

你應該打電話給他們。

舉一反三 **Useful Sentences**

➲ **請介紹可以去的地方**

01 **Where's a good place to visit?**
有什麼地方好玩？

02 **Do you know of a good hotel in Taipei?**
你知道台北有哪一家旅館較好嗎？

03 **Spain is really beautiful to visit.**
西班牙很漂亮，值得去玩。

重要英語單字 **Vocabulary**

mood →心情

pizza →匹薩餅

price [praɪs] →價格

reasonable [ˈriznəbl̩] →合理的

hotel [hoˈtɛl] →旅館；飯店

tons [tʌnz] → （口語）很多

Unit 40

請介紹好的美容師

會話 1 **Dialogue 1**

MP3 41

A Mary, where's a good place to get your hair cut?

瑪莉，有哪一家美容院較好？

B I always go to Jane.

我都是找珍恩。

She works at Beauty.

她在『美麗』美容院上班。

A Does she do a good job?

她做得很好嗎？

B I think so.

我覺得不錯。

I've gone to her for 2 years.

我給她做了兩年了。

A OK, will you give me her number?

好吧，你可以把她的電話號碼給我嗎？

B It's 273-4365.

是273-4365。

Tell her I told you to call.

告訴她是我叫你打電話給她的。

會話 2 **Dialogue 2**

Ⓐ John, where do you get your hair cut?

約翰，你都在哪裡剪頭髮？

Ⓑ I usually go to Lee's Barber Shop.

我通常都去『李氏』理髮廳。

They're over by the park.

他們是在公園旁邊。

Ⓐ How much do they charge?

他們收多少錢？

Ⓑ They charge me $150.

他們都收我一百五十元。

But I always get my hair shampooed.

但我都有請他們幫我洗頭髮。

Ⓐ I wouldn't need that.

我不需要他們幫我洗頭髮。

Ⓑ Well, I think it's about $100 then.

嗯，那麼，我想大約要一百元。

舉一
反三 **Useful Sentences**

⊃ 請介紹好的理髮師

01 Where's a good place to get your hair cut?
到那一家理髮廳剪頭髮較好？

02 Where do you get your hair cut?
你都去哪裡剪頭髮？

03 Do you know of a good barber?
你知道哪一個理髮師較好嗎？

⊃ 介紹理髮師

01 There is a good barber right by your house.
你家旁邊就有一個好的理髮師。

02 I usually go to Lee's Barber Shop.
我通常都去『李氏』理髮廳。

03 I always go to Jane.
我都是找珍恩。

重要英語單字 Vocabulary

barber [ˈbɑrbɚ] →理髮師

barber shop →理髮院

charge →收費

shampooed [ʃæmˈpud] →讓人洗頭（shampoo的過去分詞）

英語會話的喜怒哀樂

用英語來抱怨

Dialogue 1

🅐 How's everything?
一切都好嗎？

🅑 Well, this burger is actually a little bit overdone.
嗯，這個漢堡煮得真有點過熟。

🅐 Can I bring you another burger?
我另外拿一個漢堡給你，好嗎？

🅑 That would be fine.
好的。

🅐 I'll take this back to the kitchen.
我把這個拿回去廚房。

And I'll have the new one out in just a moment.
我馬上拿一個新的出來給你。

🅑 Thanks.
謝謝。

會話 2 ➤ Dialogue 2

Ⓐ John, could you come here, please?
約翰，你過來一下好嗎？

Ⓑ Yes, what is it?
好的，什麼事？

Ⓐ Well, this report just doesn't cut it.
你這份報告並沒有把問題作深入研究。

You left out the entire section on food.
整個關於食物的部分你都遺漏了。

Ⓑ I'm sorry. I must have overlooked it.
很抱歉，我一定是把它忽略了。

Let me fix it.
我會把它改好。

Ⓐ OK, but I need it by five.
好，不過我五點以前要。

Ⓑ Yes sir. I'll have it for you by then.
是，先生。我會在五點以前給你。

舉一反三 ➤ Useful Sentences

➲ 你有不滿時，如何用英語表達

01 I wish you hadn't done that.
我多希望你沒有這麼做。

Chapter 10

02 **It was supposed to be ready last week.**
這件事上星期就應該做好的。

03 **I've had enough of it.**
我受夠了。

重要英語單字　Vocabulary

actually [ˈæktʃʊəlɪ] →實際上

overdone →煮得過熟

kitchen [ˈkɪtʃən] →廚房

report [rɪˈport] →報告

entire [ɪnˈtaɪr] →整個

section [ˈsɛkʃən] →（文章的）段落

overlook [ˌovɚˈlʊk] →忽略

每天開口說一句

用英語表達失望

Ⓐ What's wrong?
怎麼了？

Ⓑ Oh, I guess I'm just disappointed that Mary isn't coming over.
喔，我想我只是因為瑪莉不來，有一點失望而已。

Ⓐ I'm sorry.
唉呀，怎麼會這樣？

Is there anything I can do?
有什麼需要我幫忙的嗎？

Ⓑ No, not really.
不用，也沒什麼。

Ⓐ OK, but let me know if you need anything.
好的，但如果你需要什麼，要跟我說。

Ⓑ All right, I will.
好的，我會。

Chapter 10

會話 2 Dialogue 2

Ⓐ What's wrong?

怎麼啦？

Ⓑ Nothing.

沒什麼

Ⓐ Come on, you can tell me.

別這樣，你可以跟我說。

Ⓑ Well, I was expecting to have a paycheck this Friday.

嗯，我本來期待這個星期五領薪水。

They said it wouldn't be in until Monday.

他們卻說要到下星期一才發薪水。

Ⓐ I'm sorry.

我很同情你。

Are you mad?

你很生氣嗎？

Ⓑ No, I'm just disappointed.

也不是，我只是感到失望。

舉一
反三　**Useful Sentences**

➲ 失望時，如何用英語表達

01 I'm disappointed in you.
我對你很失望。

02 I'm just disappointed.
我只是感到失望。

03 I was looking forward to it.
我原本是很期待的。

04 It's a shame that we couldn't go.
真倒楣，我們不能去。

05 It's not what I expected.
那不是我所期待的。

重要英語單字 Vocabulary

disappointed [dɪsə'pɔɪntɪd] →失望（disappoint的過去分詞）

expecting [ɪk'spɛktɪŋ] →期待；等（expect的現在分詞）

shame [ʃem] →（口語）倒楣事

paycheck →薪水

mad →生氣

用英語向人致歉

Dialogue 1

Ⓐ Mary, I'm sorry about last night.

瑪莉，昨晚的事我很抱歉。

Ⓑ Oh, that's OK.

喔，沒關係。

Ⓐ I never expected that we would get back that late.

我沒想到我們會那麼晚才回來。

Ⓑ Well, **some things just happen.**

嗯，有些事就是會發生，沒法子。

Ⓐ **That's true.**

那倒也是。

Please tell your dad that I'm sorry.

請跟你父親說我很抱歉。

Ⓑ Sure. I think he'll understand.

好的。我想他會明白的。

會話 **2** Dialogue 2

Ⓐ Mary, I need to talk to you.
瑪莉，我需要跟妳談談。

Ⓑ Is it about the tickets?
是關於那些票的事嗎？

Ⓐ Yes.
是的。

I'm really sorry that I didn't invite you to the game.
很抱歉我沒有邀妳去看球賽。

I thought you already had plans.
我以為妳你有其他的約會了。

Ⓑ Oh, you did?
你真是這麼想？

Ⓐ Yes, I thought your mom said you were going to Jane's house.
是啊，我以為妳母親說妳要去珍恩家。

Ⓑ Well, thanks for apologizing.
嗯，你道歉就好了，謝謝。

Maybe we can go some other time.
或許改天我們可以去。

舉一
反三

Useful Sentences

➲ 有人跟你抱怨，你怎麼回答

01	I'm sorry. 我很抱歉。
02	I apologize. 我向你道歉。
03	I'm sorry. I didn't realize... 對不起，我沒有想到……
04	Oh, I didn't know it bothered you. 喔，我不知道那會吵到你。
05	I'm sorry. I shouldn't have done it. 對不起，我不該那麼做的。

重要英語單字 Vocabulary

late →很晚

happen ['hæpən] →發生

understand [ˌʌndɚ'stænd] →瞭解；明白

invite [ɪn'vaɪt] →邀請

apologizing [ə'pɑlədʒaɪzɪŋ] →道歉（apologize的現在分詞）

bother ['bɑθɚ] →困擾

realize ['rɪə,laɪz] →想到

Unit 44

生氣時，如何用英語表達

會話 1 **Dialogue 1**

 MP3 45

A John, come here right now!
約翰，立刻到這裡來。

B I'm coming.
來了。

A Sit down!
坐下。

You're in trouble.
你惹麻煩了。

B Why?
為什麼？

A Mrs. Lin called and said that you cheated on your test today.
林老師打電話來，說你今天考試作弊。

You have some apologizing to do.
你必須要道歉。

B I'm sorry. I shouldn't have done it.
對不起，我不該這麼做。

I'll tell her I'm sorry tomorrow.
明天我會跟她道歉。

I'm really sorry.

我真的很抱歉。

會話 2 **Dialogue 2**

（約翰打弟弟，被媽媽看到…）

A John, stop that right now!

約翰，現在馬上住手。

Come here immediately!

立刻到這裡來。

B What?

有什麼事嗎？

A **Don't take that tone with me!**

別給我裝得一副很無辜的調調。

I saw you hit your brother.

我看見你打你弟弟。

B No! He hit me first.

不！是他先打我的。

A **I don't care.**

我不管。

You know better than to hit him.

你知道你不該打他的。

Go sit on your bed for ten minutes.

到你房間床上去靜坐十分鐘。

B OK.
好。

舉一反三 **Useful Sentences**

⊃ 生氣時

01	That makes me mad. 那令我很生氣。
02	I can't stand it. 我受不了。
03	I am upset. 我很生氣。
04	I'm not very happy about this. 我對這件事不太高興。
04	I'm very mad. 我很生氣。

重要英語單字 Vocabulary

trouble [ˈtrʌbl̩] →麻煩

cheated [ˈtʃitɪd] →考試作弊（cheat的過去式）

immediately [ɪˈmidɪˌɪtlɪ] →立刻

tone [ton] →語調

hit [hɪt] →打

stand →忍受

Chapter 10

Unit 45
用英語表達悲傷

會話 1 Dialogue 1

Ⓐ What's wrong?
怎麼啦？

Ⓑ My girlfriend just broke up with me.
我的女朋友跟我分手了。

I can't believe it.
我真不能相信有這種事。

Ⓐ I'm sorry.
唉呀，怎麼會呢？

Can I do anything for you?
有什麼事要我做嗎？

Ⓑ Bring me a box of tissue.
拿一盒紙巾給我。

I'm crying all over myself.
我已經哭得一塌糊塗。

Ⓐ Here you go.
紙巾在這兒。

Ⓑ I can't believe it.
我真不敢相信有這種事。

This is the worst thing that ever happened to me.

這是我遇到過最倒楣的事。

會話 2 **Dialogue 2**

（回家向媽媽哭訴…）

Ⓐ Mommy!

媽咪！

Ⓑ What is it?

什麼事？

Ⓐ Mommy, John said he didn't like me anymore.

媽咪！約翰説他不再喜歡我了。

Ⓑ Oh, you know he's just saying that.

哦，你知道他只是説説而已。

He'll be here in ten minutes to ask you to play.

再過十分鐘他就會來邀你出去玩。

Ⓐ But he makes me cry.

但是他惹我哭了。

Ⓑ I know.

我知道。

Everything will be all right.

一切都會沒事的。

Come here and give me a hug.

過來給我抱一下。

30秒破解英語會話

　　美國人常喜歡跟小孩子說「給我抱一下」，它的英語說法就是Give me a hug. 每當有人遇到不如意的事情時，我們常會安慰對方說「往好處想」，它的英語說法就是Look on the bright side.

舉一反三　**Useful Sentences**

⊃ 有人遭遇困難，你如何安慰他

01	I'm sorry. 我很遺憾。
02	That's too bad. 那真是糟糕。
03	Look on the bright side. 往好處想。
04	It's not the end of the world. 那也不是世界末日。
03	Don't worry. Things will get better. 別擔心，事情總會好轉的。
04	Everything will be all right. 一切都會沒事的。

重要英語單字　Vocabulary

tissue [tɪʃʊ] →紙巾
hug [hʌg] →擁抱
bright [braɪt] →明亮的
worry [ˈwɝɪ] →擔心

如何用英語表示漠不關心

Dialogue 1

MP3 47

Ⓐ Where do you want to eat?

你要去哪裡吃飯？

Ⓑ I don't care.

我隨便都可以。

Ⓐ Do you want Japanese food, Chinese food…

你要吃日本料理，中國菜還是…

Ⓑ I really don't care.

我真的都沒關係。

Whatever you want is fine with me.

你要吃什麼我都可以。

Ⓐ All right, then we'll just eat here.

好吧，那我們在這兒吃就行。

I've got some hot dogs in the fridge.

我冰箱裡有一些熱狗。

Ⓑ OK. That's fine with me.

好。那也可以。

會話 2 **Dialogue 2**

Ⓐ Do you like the blue one or the red one better?

你比較喜歡這個藍色的，還是紅色的？

Ⓑ Either one.

哪一個都可以。

Ⓐ Well, which one would you pick?

那，你會挑哪一個？

Ⓑ I don't know.

我沒意見。

I like them both.

兩個我都喜歡。

Ⓐ Are you sure you don't know?

你真的沒意見？

Ⓑ I'm positive.

確實沒意見。

Either one is fine.

哪一個都可以？

30秒破解英語會話

care這個字就是「在乎」的意思，所以你常聽美國人說I don't care.也就是「無所謂」的意思。

另一種說法是，「某件事is fine.或is fine with me.」表示「沒有關係」，也就是「我都無所謂」的意思。

舉一
反三　　**Useful Sentences**

● 表示都無所謂，英語怎麼說

01　I don't care.
我不在乎。

02　Whatever you like.
你喜歡的就行。

03　Do whatever you like.
你喜歡怎麼做就怎麼做。

04　Either one.
哪一個都可以。

05　It doesn't matter to me.
我沒關係。

06　I don't care much about one way or another.
這樣做或那樣做，我都不在乎。

重要英語單字　Vocabulary

fridge [frɪdʒ] →冰箱

positive [ˈpɑzətɪv] →確信的；有把握的

pick →挑選

care →在乎

matter [ˈmætɚ] →要緊；有關係

Chapter 10

Unit 47
如何用英語表示驚訝

會話
1
Dialogue 1

MP3
48

（送男朋友生日禮物）

A John, here you go.
約翰，拿去。

B What is it?
是什麼？

A Open it.
打開。

B OK.
好的。

A watch?
一支手錶？

I can't believe it!
我真不敢相信。

You got me a watch!
妳為我買了一支手錶。

A Happy Birthday!
祝你生日快樂。

B I can't believe it.

我真不敢相信。

This is awesome!

這太棒了。

會話 2 **Dialogue 2**

A Mary, I have something for you.

瑪莉，我有東西給你。

B What is it?

是什麼？

A It's a check.

是一張支票。

This will cover all of your hospital bills.

足夠你付清所有欠醫院的錢。

B What? Wow, thank you!

什麼？噢，謝謝你。

I can't believe it!

我真不敢相信。

A Well, **I knew that you were struggling.**

嗯，我知道你有困難。

And I just wanted to help out.

我只是想幫你一點忙。

B I never expected this.

這太出我意料之外了。

Thank you so much.

非常、非常感謝你。

你覺得驚訝時，英語怎麼說

01	I can't believe it. 我真不敢相信。
02	Really? 真的？
03	Don't be kidding! 別開玩笑了！
04	Oh, what's that? 嘎，那是什麼？
05	Oh, dear! 啊，天啊！
06	Oh, my. 噢，我的天哪！
07	What? 什麼！
08	Oh, my gosh! 哎呀，我的媽呀！

重要英語單字 Vocabulary

watch →手錶

awesome ['ɔsəm] →（口語）很棒的

hospital ['hɑspɪtl̩] →醫院

bill →帳單

struggling ['strʌglɪŋ] →困鬥（struggle的現在分詞）

每天開口說一句

如何用英語表示關懷

會話 1 Dialogue 1

Ⓐ Mary, what are you doing?
瑪莉，妳在做什麼？

Ⓑ I'm getting ready to go to John's.
我正準備要去約翰家。

Ⓐ I'm a little worried about you seeing him.
我有點擔心妳跟他交往。

Ⓑ Oh , Dad.
喔，爸爸。

Ⓐ Well, he just scares me a little.
哪，他只是有點嚇到我。

Just promise me that you'll be careful. OK?
答應我妳會小心。好嗎？

Ⓑ I will.
我會的。

I'll call you if anything happens.
如果有什麼事我會打電話給你。

I promise.
我一定會的。

會話 2 **Dialogue 2**

A Hi, John.
嗨，約翰。

B Hi, Mary.
嗨，瑪莉。

I need to ask you something.
有一件事我要問妳。

A **OK, shoot.**
好的，講吧。

B Well, this isn't easy for me to say, but I think I have to.
嗯，這件事我要說出來不容易，但是我想我必須說。

I think you need to watch how you're spending your money.
我認為妳花錢應該小心。

I'm worried that you're going to be broke within a month.
我擔心妳一個月就把錢花光了。

A Well, I think you're right.
嗯，我認為你是對的。

I've been concerned, too.
我一直也在擔心。

Chapter 10

I just needed to hear it from someone.
我只是要有人點醒我。

I'll be more careful from now on.
從現在起我會小心一點。

Ⓑ Good, and if you need any advice, just ask.
好的,如果妳需要任何建議,儘管問。

舉一反三 **Useful Sentences**

⊃ 關懷對方

01 What's the matter?
怎麼啦?

02 What's the matter with you?
你怎麼啦?

03 What's wrong?
有什麼事嗎?

04 What happened?
發生了什麼事?

05 What's going on?
有什麼事?

06 Are you all right?
你沒事吧?

07	Are you Okay? 你沒事吧？
08	Is everything all right? 一切都好嗎？
09	How do you feel about that? 那件事你覺得怎麼樣？

重要英語單字　Vocabulary

worried ['wɜɪd] →擔心的

scare →使害怕

promise ['prɑmɪs] →答應

spending ['spɛndɪŋ] →花錢

broke →沒有錢

concerned [kən'sɜnd] →擔心的

advice →勸告

Chapter 10

Unit 49

如何用英語說你不舒服

 會話 1 **Dialogue 1**

 MP3 50

Ⓐ John, do we have any cold medicine?
約翰，我們有感冒藥嗎？

Ⓑ Well sure.
嗯，有的。

What's wrong?
怎麼啦？

Ⓐ My head hurts and my throat is sore.
我頭很疼而且喉嚨也痛。

Ⓑ We have some Vick's in the kitchen.
廚房裡有Vick's。

It should work.
應該管用。

Ⓐ Would you get it for me?
你可以幫我拿嗎？

Ⓑ Sure, I'll be right back.
好的，我馬上來。

會話 2 **Dialogue 2**

Ⓐ Honey, I don't feel good.
親愛的，我覺得不舒服。

Ⓑ Do you want some medicine?
你要什麼藥嗎？

Ⓐ No, not really.
不，並不需要。

I just want to go to sleep.
我只需要睡一下。

Ⓑ OK, I'll get the bed ready for you.
好吧，我替你把床鋪好。

Do you want something to drink?
你要喝點什麼嗎？

Ⓐ Do we have orange juice?
我們有柳橙汁嗎？

Ⓑ Yes, I'll bring you some.
有，我去拿一些給你。

30秒破解英語會話

　　當我們要説，家裡有哪種藥時，直接把藥名説出來，例如：We have some Vick's in the kitchen.（廚房裡有Vick's），這句話中的Vick's就是一種感冒藥的名字。

舉一反三　Useful Sentences

⊃ 你覺得不舒服時，英語怎麼說

01 **I don't feel very well.**
我覺得不舒服。

02 **I feel sick.**
我覺得不舒服。

03 **I think I have a cold.**
我想我感冒了。

04 **My stomach hurts.**
我的胃會痛。

05 **I think I'm getting sick.**
我想我是病了。

⊃ 有人不舒服時，你怎麼回答

01 **What's wrong?**
怎麼啦？

02 **Do you want some medicine?**
你要吃什麼藥嗎？

03	**What do you want me to do?** 你要我怎麼做？
04	**Do you want to go to the doctor?** 你要去看醫生嗎？
05	**Maybe you should rest for a while.** 或許你應該休息一會兒。

重要英語單字 Vocabulary

cold →感冒
medicine [ˈmɛdəsn̩] →藥
hurt [hɝt] →痛
sore [sor] →痛
throat [θrot] →喉嚨
stomach [ˈstɑmək] →胃

Chapter 10

敘述事情的英語會話

Dialogue 1

🅐 So, I hear you're getting married.
嘿，我聽說你要結婚了。

🅑 Yes, I'm getting married on June 14.
是的，我六月十四要結婚。

Have you ever met John?
你見過約翰沒？

🅐 No, I don't think I have.
沒有，我想我沒見過。

🅑 Oh, you'd like him.
喔，你會喜歡他的。

We still have to plan the wedding.
我們還在為婚禮做準備。

🅐 What do you have to do?
你們還有哪些事要做？

🅑 Well, we need to pick out the flowers and the music.
嗯，我們需要挑選花和音樂。

And, we have to decide on the tuxedos.

還有，西裝我們也還沒選好。

It is fun though, so I don't mind doing it.

不過這些很好玩，所以我不介意做這些事。

會話 2 Dialogue 2

Ⓐ When do you want to take our vacation?

你計畫我們何時去度假？

Ⓑ I was thinking that we could go in February.

我在想我們二月可以去。

Does that sound good?

你聽起來認為好嗎？

Ⓐ Sure, do you think you can get off work in February?

當然好，你想你二月可以請假嗎？

Ⓑ Yes, but we'd need to go on a Friday instead of Thursday.

可以，但我們必須在星期五離開，而不是星期四。

We could stay until Tuesday.

我們可以玩到星期二。

Ⓐ That will work.

那沒問題。

I'll call the hotel tomorrow.

明天我會打電話去訂旅館。

Ⓑ Great, I can't wait!
好棒，我等不及了。

舉一反三 **Useful Sentences**

⮑ 問對方的計畫

01 So, I hear you're getting married.
嘿，我聽說你要結婚了。

02 I heard that you're going to move.
我聽說你要搬家了。

03 Do you have everything planned for your wedding?
你的婚禮一切都計畫好了嗎？

04 What are you going to do at the party?
在宴會上你要做什麼？

05 Where are you going on vacation?
你要去哪裡度假？

⮑ 告訴別人你的計畫

01 Yah, we're getting married in a couple of weeks.
是啊，我們再過兩星期就要結婚了。

02 We're moving to New York.
我們要搬到紐約。

03 We're still planning the move.
我們還在準備搬家。

04 We've got to save some money for our vacation.
我們必須存些錢去度假。

05 We want to play some games at the party.
宴會上我們想玩些遊戲。

06 We're taking a trip to Europe.
我們要到歐洲旅行。

重要英語單字 Vocabulary

move →搬家

wedding ['wɛdɪŋ] →婚禮

vacation [və'keʃən] →假期

save →節省

tuxedo [tʌk'sido] →男性正式西裝禮服

mind →介意

Chapter 11

 Dialogue 1

Ⓐ When are you going to apply for school?
你什麼時候要申請學校？

Ⓑ In August.
八月。

They start accepting applications then.
他們那時開始接受申請。

Ⓐ **That's odd.**
那就怪了。

It seems like they should start earlier.
他們似乎應該早一點開始。

Ⓑ Well, the applications in August are actually for the following year.
嗯，八月開始的申請事實上是為明年申請的。

Ⓐ **Oh, I see.**
喔，我明白了。

So you'll start next year.
所以你明年入學。

Ⓑ Yes, if everything goes as planned.
是的，如果一切按計畫進行的話。

會話 2 — Dialogue 2

Ⓐ So, I hear you're graduating in a couple of weeks.

嘿，我聽說你再兩個星期就畢業了。

Ⓑ Yah, **I'm pretty excited.**

是啊，我很興奮。

Ⓐ What are you going to do after that?

畢業後你要做什麼？

Ⓑ Well, I'm moving back home for two weeks.

我要先搬回家兩個星期。

Then I'm getting married on the 14th.

然後，我十四號要結婚。

Ⓐ Wow, I didn't know that!

唉呀，我不知道耶。

Congratulations and best wishes.

恭禧！祝你幸福。

Ⓑ Thanks a lot.

多謝。

重要英語單字　Vocabulary

apply [ə'plaɪ] →申請

application [æplə'keʃən] →申請表；申請

odd →奇怪的

following →接著的

congratulations [kən,grætʃə'leʃənz] →恭禧

說一件過去的事

會話 1 Dialogue 1

🅐 Mary, do you remember when we met?
瑪莉，妳還記得我們認識的時候嗎？

🅑 I won't ever forget it.
我永遠不會忘記。

I was sitting in the cafeteria all by myself...
那時，我一個人自己坐在自助餐廳……

🅐 And I came up and asked to sit by you...
而我走過來，要求坐在妳旁邊……

🅑 Oh, it seems like it was just yesterday.
喔，那好像是昨天剛發生的事一般。

🅐 Just think, now we've been married for five years.
想想看，現在我們已經結婚五年了。

🅑 **That was one of the best days of my life.**
那天是我一生中最快樂的日子之一。

Ⓐ John, do you remember that video we made one summer while we were in high school?

約翰，你還記得我們在高中的時候，有個夏天錄製的錄影帶嗎？

Ⓑ Are you kidding?

開什麼玩笑？

I watched that the other day.

我前幾天還在看。

Ⓐ That was so funny!

那時真滑稽！

Ⓑ Yah, that was about the only thing fun that whole summer.

是啊，那大約是那年夏天唯一好玩的事了。

Ⓐ We ought to make another one some time.

我們有空應該再錄製一個。

Ⓑ OK. Let's do it now.

好啊。我們現在就做。

舉一
反三 **Useful Sentences**

➲ 提起過去的事情

01 **Do you remember when we met?**
你還記得我們認識的時候嗎？

02	Do you remember our 10th grade English teacher? 你還記得我們十年級的英文老師嗎？
03	Remember that song we used to sing? 你還記得我們過去常唱的那首歌嗎？
04	Wasn't it so fun last year? 去年不是很好玩嗎？
05	Don't you just love talking about old times? 談過去的時光讓人覺得真舒暢啊？

⊃ 想起美好的往日

01	I'll never forget when we met. 我永遠也不會忘記我們相遇的時候。
02	I'll always remember that. 我會永遠記得。
03	That was such a fun time. 那段時間真的很好玩哪。
04	I wish I could do it all over again. 我多希望可以再從頭來一回。

重要英語單字 Vocabulary

remember [rɪˈmɛmbɚ] →記得

forget [fɚˈgɛt] →忘記

cafeteria [ˌkæfəˈtɪrɪə] →自助餐廳

video →錄影帶

會話 1 Dialogue 1

A I hear you got a new car.

我聽說你買了一部新車。

What does it look like?

什麼樣子的？

B It's an 84 Buick.

是84年的別克車。

It's blue with leather interior.

是藍色的，內部是皮的。

A Does it have a stereo?

有沒有音響？

B Yah, it's got a CD, tape player, and an AM / FM radio.

有，有CD、錄音機和AM/FM收音機。

A That's cool!

那好棒！

B Plus, it has power windows and locks.

還有，它有全自動窗和全自動鎖。

I like it a lot.

我非常喜歡它。

會話 2 **Dialogue 2**

Ⓐ John, are we going to buy that house you were looking at?

約翰，我們要買你去看的那棟房子嗎？

Ⓑ Well, I'm not sure.

嗯，我還沒決定。

Ⓐ What does it look like?

房子是什麼樣子？

Ⓑ I think you'd love it.

我想你會喜歡。

It has 4 bedrooms, 2 baths, 2 living rooms, and huge closets!

那棟房子有四房，兩個浴室，兩間客廳，衣櫥很大。

Ⓐ What about a pool?

那游泳池呢？

Does it have a pool?

沒有游泳池？

Ⓑ You bet.

那還用說？

It's huge.

游泳池很大。

It will be fun if we buy it!

如果我們買了會很好玩。

舉一反三 **Useful Sentences**

➜ 問某人或某件東西的樣子

01 What does your car look like?
你的車子是什麼樣子？

02 Tell me about your house.
告訴我你的房子的樣子。

03 What does John look like?
約翰是什麼樣子？

04 How tall is John?
約翰多高？

05 What kind of equipment does it have?
它有什麼配備？

➜ 形容某人或某件東西的樣子

01 It is blue with leather interior.
是藍色的，內部是皮的。

02 It is a 3-story house, and it has 5 bedrooms.
是三層樓的房子，有五間房間。

03 She's tall, has blonde hair, and is really skinny.
她很高，金黃色的頭髮，很瘦。

Chapter 11

04	He has blonde hair. 他有金黃色的頭髮。
05	He's 6 feet tall. 他六呎高。

重要英語單字　Vocabulary

leather [ˈlɛðɚ] →皮革

interior [ɪnˈtɪrɪɚ] →內部

closet →衣櫥

equipment [ɪˈkwɪpmənt] →設備

每天開口說一句

購物英語

Unit 54
買衣服需用到的英語

 會話 1 **Dialogue 1**

 MP3 55

A Hi, can I help you?
嗨，你有什麼事嗎？

B Sure, I'm looking for a pair of jeans for my daughter.
有，我在替我女兒找一件牛仔褲。

A What size does she wear?
她穿幾號的？

B Either 6 or 8, depending upon the cut of the jeans.
六號或八號，要看牛仔褲的剪裁。

A OK, we have several different styles in those sizes right around the corner.
好，那種尺寸我們有好幾種不同樣式，放在轉角處那兒。

Let me know if I can help you any more.
如果你還需要其他的幫忙，讓我知道。

B OK, thanks a lot.
好的，謝謝你。

會話 2 **Dialogue 2**

A Hello, welcome to David's Men's Store.
哈囉，歡迎光臨『大衛』男士服飾店。

How can I help you today?
今天你要買什麼嗎？

B I'm looking for a new suit.
我在找新西裝。

A Do you know what size you need?
你知道你要的尺寸嗎？

B No, I'm not sure.
不，我不知道。

I'd like to be measured, please.
請幫我量一量。

A OK, it looks like you need about a 48 long jacket.
好的，看來你西裝上衣大約要48吋長。

And your waist is 36.
你的腰圍是36吋。

Which colors are you interested in?
你要買什麼顏色的？

B I'd like to see one in black and another in brown.
我想看看一件黑色的，另一件棕色的。

Thanks a lot.

謝謝你。

重要英語單字 Vocabulary

jeans →牛仔褲

style →樣式；型式

measured [mɛˈʒɚd] →量衣服（measure的過去分詞）

waist [west] →腰圍

每天開口說一句

Unit 55

買鞋子需用到的英語

Dialogue 1

MP3 56

A Hi, I need a pair of shoes for work.
嗨，我上班需要一雙鞋子。

B Where do you work?
你在哪裡上班？

A At an office, so they need to be dressy.
是在一個寫字樓裡，所以我要正式一點的鞋子。

I wear size 10.
我穿十號。

B OK, I'll bring out a few different pairs in size 10 and let you try them on.
好的，我會拿幾雙不同型式的十號鞋子來，讓你試穿。

A Sure. Maybe something with laces.
好的。最好是有鞋帶的。

B Yes, sir.
好的，先生。

I'll be right back.
我馬上拿來。

會話 2 Dialogue 2

Ⓐ May I help you?

你需要我幫忙嗎?

Ⓑ Yes, I'm trying to find a pair of shoes for my son.

是的,我正在幫我兒子找一雙鞋子。

He needs some cleats for football.

他打美式足球需要釘鞋。

Ⓐ Do you know his shoe size?

你知道他穿幾號鞋嗎?

Ⓑ He wears size 8.

他穿八號的。

Ⓐ OK, we have any of the cleats on the left wall in size 8.

好的,我們所有八號釘鞋都放在左邊的牆上。

Ⓑ Thank you.

謝謝你。

重要英語單字 Vocabulary

dressy [ˈdrɛsɪ] →正式的

pair →一雙

lace →鞋帶

cleats [klits] →釘鞋

Unit 56

買眼鏡需用到的英語

Dialogue 1

Ⓐ Hello, I need new contacts.
哈囉，我需要新的隱形眼鏡。

Ⓑ Do you need to have your eyes examined?
你需要驗光嗎？

Ⓐ Yes, I do.
是的，需要。

Do you carry disposable lenses?
你們有用完即丟的鏡片嗎？

Ⓑ We sure do.
我們有。

We have a special which includes the eye exam and your lenses for six weeks.
我們有項特價，包括驗光和六星期份的鏡片。

The price is $5200.
價錢是五千兩百元。

Ⓐ OK, I may be interested in that.
好的，我可能對那個有興趣。

B All right, just fill out these forms for me and we'll get started.

好，請把這些表格填好，我們就可以開始。

會話 2 — Dialogue 2

A Hello, thank you for calling The Glasses Store.

哈囉，謝謝你打電話來『眼鏡店』。

Can I help you?

有什麼事嗎？

B Yes, I'm interested in getting new glasses.

有，我要買新眼鏡。

Do you have any specials right now?

你們現在有什麼特價優待嗎？

A Yes, we do.

有的。

One pair of glasses is $990.

一副眼鏡是九百九十元。

You can purchase a second pair of glasses for only $490.

你再買第二副是四百九十元。

B Does that price include an eye exam?

那個價錢包括驗光嗎？

Ⓐ Yes,it does.

是的，包括。

The lenses are plastic.

鏡片是塑膠鏡片。

If you prefer glass lenses, they are an additional $300 per pair.

如果你要玻璃鏡片，每副要多加三百元。

Ⓑ OK, thanks for the information.

好的，謝謝你告訴我這些。

I might come by tonight. Bye.

我今天晚上可能會來。再見。

重要英語單字 Vocabulary

contact [ˈkɑntækt] →隱形眼鏡

disposable [dɪsˈpozəbl̩] →用後即丟棄的

lens →鏡片

special →特價優待

form [fɔrm] →表格

plastic [ˈplæstɪk] →塑膠的

additional [əˈdɪʃənəl] →額外的；另外的

Unit 57

買飾物和香水需用到的英語

會話 1 **Dialogue 1**

MP3 58

Ⓐ Hi, welcome to the Belt Outlet.

嗨，歡迎光臨『皮帶賣場』。

Can I help you today?

需要我幫忙嗎？

Ⓑ Sure.

是的。

I need a belt that is kind of casual and kind of dressy.

我需要一條腰帶，不要太隨意也不要太正式。

Ⓐ Hmm, perhaps a leather belt would work.

嗯，也許皮製腰帶還可以應付得上。

Do you prefer lighter or darker colors?

你喜歡淡一點的顏色還是深一點的？

Ⓑ I like darker colors.

我喜歡深一點的顏色。

Maybe a brown.

也許棕色的吧。

A OK, here are a few different styles.
好的，這裡有一些不同型式的。

I'll let you look at them.
我讓你看看。

If you need anything else, just let me know.
如果你還需要其他的，跟我說一聲。

B All right, thanks a lot.
好的，謝謝你。

會話
2 Dialogue 2

A Hi, I'm looking for some perfume for my wife.
嗨，我要買香水給我太太。

B What do you have in mind?
你要買哪一類的？

A I'd like something that's not too strong.
我要味道不會太濃的。

She likes softer smelling perfume.
她喜歡味道淡一點的香水。

B OK, here are three different bottles.
好的，這裡有三種不同的瓶子。

Which one of these do you like?
你喜歡哪一個？

A Let me see... Oooh, I like that!

讓我看看……嗯，我喜歡那個。

What is it called?

那個香水叫什麼？

B That's Poison.

它是叫做『毒藥』的香水。

It comes in a 4 ounce bottle and a 6 ounce bottle.

有四盎司裝的，也有六盎司裝的。

> **重要英語單字** Vocabulary

casual [ˈkæʒʊəl] →日常便服的；不正式的

perfume [pɚˈfjum] →香水

bottle →瓶

prefer [prɪˈfɝ] →較喜歡

perhaps →或許

買珠寶需用到的英語

**MP3
59**

Ⓐ Hi, welcome to the Diamond Store.
嗨，歡迎光臨『鑽石店』。

How can I help you?
需要我幫忙嗎？

Ⓑ I'm looking for an engagement ring for my girlfriend.
我要買一個訂婚戒指給我的女朋友。

Ⓐ What type of cut do you like for the diamond?
你要切成什麼形狀的鑽石？

Ⓑ I want a round stone in the center.
我要中間是圓形的鑽石。

But, I would also like some baguettes on both sides of the center stone.
但是，我還要一些狹長型的鑽石放在中間圓形鑽石的兩旁。

Ⓐ She sure must be special!
她一定是個很特別的女孩。

Let me show you this ring.
讓我拿這個戒指給你看。

It sounds just like what you're looking for.

它就像你在找的。

B All right, I'll take a look.

好的，讓我看看。

會話
2
Dialogue 2

A Hi, I'm looking for a new watch.

嗨，我要買新手錶。

I want something that is pretty nice but isn't really expensive.

我要好看但是價錢不要太貴那種。

B How much are you wanting to spend?

你打算花多少錢買？

A Oh, about $1000 to $1500.

喔，大約一千到一千五百元。

B We have several in that range.

那個價位的錶我們有好幾個。

Here's a watch by Citizen that is really unique.

這裡有一只很別緻的星辰表。

The band is gold plated and the face has one diamond in the center.

錶帶是鍍金的，錶面有一個鑽石在中央。

Would you like to try this one on?

你要不要戴戴看？

A Yah, I really like that.

好啊，我很喜歡。

Oooh, it fits nice!

唔，戴起來恰恰好。

How much is it?

多少錢？

B This one is normally $1700 but it's on sale for $1200.

這只通常是賣一千七百元，但是現在在打折優待只賣一千兩百元。

It's a great deal!

是很好的價錢。

舉一反三 | **Useful Sentences**

➔ 店員招呼顧客的話

01 Can I help you?
能為您服務嗎？

02 May I help you?
可以為您服務嗎？

03 What are you looking for?
您找的是什麼樣的東西呢？

04
Let me know if I can help you.
需要我服務的話，就招呼我一聲。

➲ 有店員過來招呼你時，你如何回答

01
I'm looking for a new watch.
我在找一個新手錶。

02
I'm just browsing, thanks.
我只是看看東西，謝謝。

03
I just want to look around.
我只要隨便看看而已。

04
Do you have any jeans on sale?
你們有牛仔褲在打折嗎？

05
I'm looking for a new suit.
我在找一套新西裝。

06
I'm trying to find a pair of shoes for my son.
我在幫我兒子找一雙鞋。

➲ 詢問價格

01
How much is this?
這個要多少錢？

➲ 店員回答顧客的詢問

01
It's on sale for $75.
它現在正在打折，賣七十五美元。

02
It's $200.
價錢是兩百美元。

● 結帳時，店員說的話

01
Will this be cash or charge?
要付現金還是用信用卡？

02
How would you like to pay for this, cash or charge?
妳要怎麼付錢，現金還是信用卡？

● 退貨

01
I'd like a refund, please.
我要退貨，把錢拿回來。

02
Is this item returnable?
這項貨品可不可以退？

重要英語單字 Vocabulary

engagement [ɪnˈgedʒmənt] →訂婚

baguette [bæˈgɛt] →狹長型寶石

diamond →鑽石

unique [juˈnik] →獨特的

band →錶帶

normally [ˈnɔrməlɪ] →通常

refund [rɪˈfʌnd] →退還

英語系列：58

30秒用英語和老外外聊不停，超簡單！

作者／施孝昌‧Scott Williams
出版者／哈福企業有限公司
地址／新北市板橋區五權街 16 號
電話／(02)2808-6545　傳真／(02) 2808-6545
郵政劃撥／31598840　戶名／哈福企業有限公司
出版日期／2019 年 7 月
定價／NT$ 299 元（附 MP3）

全球華文國際市場總代理／采舍國際有限公司
地址／新北市中和區中山路 2 段 366 巷 10 號 3 樓
電話／(02) 8245-8786　傳真／(02) 8245-8718
網址／www.silkbook.com　新絲路華文網

香港澳門總經銷／和平圖書有限公司
地址／香港柴灣嘉業街 12 號百樂門大廈 17 樓
電話／(852) 2804-6687　傳真／(852) 2804-6409
定價／港幣 100 元（附 MP3）

email／haanet68@Gmail.com

郵撥打九折，郵撥未滿 500 元，酌收 1 成運費，
滿 500 元以上者免運費

國家圖書館出版品預行編目資料

30秒用英語和老外外聊不停，超簡單！／施孝昌, Scott
Williams合著. -- 新北市：哈福出版, 2019.07
　　面；　公分. --（英語系列；58）
　　ISBN　978-986-97425-6-6（平裝附光碟片）

1.英語 2.會話

805.188